DIRTY MONEY

DIRTY MONEY

RICHARD
STARK

GRAND CENTRAL
PUBLISHING

New York   Boston

Grand Central Publishing
Hachette Book Group USA
237 Park Avenue
New York, NY 10017

Visit our Web site at www.HachetteBookGroupUSA.com.

Printed in the United States of America

First Edition: April 2008
10 9 8 7 6 5 4 3 2 1

Grand Central Publishing is a division of Hachette Book Group USA, Inc. The Grand Central Publishing name and logo is a trademark of Hachette Book Group USA, Inc.

Library of Congress Control Number: 2007931314
ISBN-13: 978-0-446-17858-7
ISBN-10: 0-446-17858-6

This is for Dr. Quirke,
and his creator—two lovely gents

DIRTY MONEY

ONE

1

When the silver Toyota Avalon bumped down the dirt road out of the woods and across the railroad tracks, Parker put the Infiniti into low and stepped out onto the gravel. The Infiniti jerked forward toward the river as the Toyota slewed around behind it to a stop. Parker picked up the full duffel bag from where he'd tossed it on the ground, and behind him, the Infiniti rolled down the slope into the river, all its windows open; it slid into the gray dawn water like a bear into a trout stream.

Parker carried the duffel in his arms and Claire got out of the Toyota to open its rear door and say, "Do you want to drive?"

"No. I've been driving." He heaved the duffel onto the backseat, then got around to take the passenger side in front.

Before getting behind the wheel, she stood looking toward the river, a tall slender ash-blonde in black slacks and a bulky dark red sweater against the October chill. "It's gone," she said.

"Good."

She slid into the Toyota then and kissed him and held his face in her slim hands. "It's been a while."

"It didn't come out the way it was supposed to."

"But you got back," she said, and steered the Toyota across the tracks and up the dirt road through scrub woods. "Was one of the men with you named Dalesia?"

"Nick. They nabbed him."

"He escaped," she said, paused at the blacktop state road and turned right, southward.

"Nick escaped?"

"I had the news on, driving up. It happened a couple of hours ago, in Boston. They were transferring him from the state police to the federal, going to take him somewhere south to question him. He killed a marshal, escaped with the gun."

Parker looked at her profile. They were almost alone on the road, not yet seven AM, she driving fast. He said, "They grabbed him yesterday. They didn't question him yet?"

"That's what they said." She shrugged, eyes on the road. "They didn't say so, but it sounded to me like a turf war, the local police and the FBI. The FBI won, but then they lost him."

Parker looked out at this hilly country road, heading south. Soon they'd be coming into New Jersey. "If nobody questioned Nick yet, then they don't know where the money is."

With a head gesture toward the duffel bag behind them, she said, "That isn't it?"

"No, that's something else."

She laughed, mostly in surprise. "You don't have that money, so you picked up some other money on the way back?"

"There was too much heat around the robbery," he told her. "We could stash it, but we couldn't carry it. We each took a little, and Nick tried to spend some of his, but they had the serial numbers."

"Oh. That's why they caught him. Do *you* have some?"

"Not any more."

"Good."

They rode in silence for a while, he stretching his legs, rolling his shoulders, a big ropy man who looked squeezed into the Toyota. He'd driven through the night, called Claire an hour ago from a diner to make the meet and get rid of the Infiniti, which was too hot and too speckled with fingerprints. Now they passed a slow-moving oil delivery truck and he said, "I need some sleep, but after that I'll want you to drive me to Long Island. All my identification got wasted in the mess in Massachusetts. I'd better not drive until I get new papers."

"You're just going to talk to somebody?"

"That's all."

"Then I can drive you."

"Good."

She watched the road; no traffic now. She said, "This is still something about the robbery?"

"The third guy with us," he said. "He'll know what it means, too, that Nick's on the loose."

"That the police don't know where the money is."

"But Nick knows where we are, or could point in a direction. Are we all still partners?" He shook his head. "You kill a lawman," he said, "you're in another zone. McWhitney and I are gonna have to work this out."

"But not on the phone."

Parker yawned. "Nothing on the phone ever," he said. "Except pizza."

2

Once or twice, Claire had gotten too close to Parker's other world, or that world had gotten too close to her, and she hadn't liked it, so he did his best to keep her separate from that kind of thing. But this business was all right; everything had already happened, this was just a little tidying up.

She drove them eastward across New Jersey late that afternoon, and he told her the situation: "There was a meeting that didn't pan out. A guy there named Harbin was a problem a lot of different ways. He was wearing a wire—"

"A police wire?"

"Which got him killed. Then it turned out there was federal reward money out on him, and it attracted a bounty hunter named Keenan."

She said, "This didn't have anything to do with you in Massachusetts."

"Nothing. This was just an annoyance, Keenan trying to find everybody at the meeting, so somebody could lead him to Harbin, which nobody was going to do. He got hold of some phone records, Nick Dalesia made two calls to our place here, that brought him around."

She glanced at him, then looked out at Interstate 80, pretty heavy traffic in both directions, a lot of big trucks, the kind of traffic where you didn't change lanes a lot. "You mean," she said, "the law might come around now, using those same records."

"I don't think so," he said. "Keenan was looking for connections. The law's looking for Nick, and they'll know he's too smart to go hole up with somebody he knows. They won't be spending time looking at phone bills."

"Well, where are we going now?"

Parker was rested, most of the day asleep, but this car still felt too small. Maybe it was because he wasn't at the wheel. He stretched in place and said, "Keenan's partner, a woman named Sandra Loscalzo, caught up with us in Massachusetts just before the job. McWhitney convinced her to go away, and when he got back to Long Island he'd lead her to Harbin."

"Who's already dead."

"Yes."

"And McWhitney lives on Long Island?"

"He's got a bar there, and lives behind it."

"And that's where we're going."

"And when we get there, the next part is up to you."

She frowned out at the traffic and the eastern sky darkening ahead of them. "Is this something I won't like?"

"I don't think so. When we get there, I can go in and talk to McWhitney and you can wait in the car, or you come in, we have a drink, it's a social occasion."

"There isn't going to be any trouble."

"None. We've got to decide what to do about Loscalzo, and we've got to decide what to do about the money. There's too much heat up in that area right now—"

"Because of what you people did."

"They're looking close at strangers," Parker said, and shrugged. "So we'll have to leave the cash where it is for a while, but if we leave it too long either they find Nick again and he trades the money for a better sentence, or he gets to it himself and cleans it out because he's desperate. Being on the run the way he is uses up a lot of cash."

"You said they have the serial numbers," she said, "so he can't use it, can he?"

"He'll leave a wide backtrail, but he won't care."

"But *you* won't be able to use it."

"Offshore," he said. "We can sell it for a percentage to people who'll take it to Africa or Asia, it'll never get into the banking system again."

"There are so many ways to do things," she said.

"There have to be."

She said, "Before, you said you have to decide what to do about what's-her-name? The bounty hunter's partner."

"Sandra Loscalzo."

"Why don't you have to decide what to do about the man? Keenan."

"He's dead, too."

"Oh."

He looked out at the traffic, which was thickening as they got closer to the city. They were both silent a while, and then he was surprised when she said, "I'll come in with you."

3

We can't go there yet, you know," McWhitney said, by way of greeting.

Standing at the bar, Parker said, "Nelson McWhitney, this is my friend Claire."

"Hello, friend," McWhitney said, and dealt two coasters onto the bar, saying, "Grab a stool. What can the house buy you?"

"I would take a scotch and soda," Claire said, as she and Parker took the two nearest stools.

"A ladies' drink," McWhitney commented. "Good. Parker?"

"Beer."

McWhitney's bar, in Bay Shore on Long Island's south shore, was deep and narrow, its dark wood walls and floors illuminated mostly by beer-sign neon. At eight-thirty on a Monday night in October it was nearly empty, two solitary men finishing whiskey along the bar and a yellow-haired woman hunched inside a black coat at the last dark table along the other side.

McWhitney himself didn't look much livelier, maybe because he too had had a rough weekend. Red-bearded and red-faced, he was a hard bulky man with a soft middle, a defensive lineman gone out of shape. He made their drinks, brought them over, and leaned close to say, "Those two will be outa here in a couple minutes, and then I'll close up."

Parker said, "What do you hear from Sandra?"

Raising an eyebrow toward Claire, McWhitney said, "Your friend's up to speed on you and me?"

"Always."

"That's nice." Nodding his head toward the rear of the bar, McWhitney said, "Sandra's not quite that good a friend, but there she is, back there, waiting on a phone call." He raised his voice: "Sandra! Look who dropped by."

When Sandra Loscalzo rose to come join them, she was tall and slender, in heels and jeans and the black coat over a dark blue sweater. She walked in a purpose-ful way, taking charge of her territory. She wasn't car-rying a glass. At the bar, she said to Parker, "The last time I saw you, you were driving a phony police car."

Parker said, "The police car was real. I was the phony. You were there?"

"Fifty-yard line." She sounded admiring, but also amused. "You boys are cute, in a destructive kind of way." Looking at Claire, she said, "Is he destructive at home?"

"Of course not," Claire said, and smiled. "I'm Claire. You're Sandra?"

"G'night, Nels," called one of the customers, rising from his seat, waving a hand over his shoulder as he left.

"See you, Norm."

Parker said to Sandra, "You're waiting for a phone call."

Sandra made a disgusted headshake and gestured at McWhitney. "This fellow and Harbin," she said. "Where's he stash him? In Ohio. *I'm* not going to Ohio, eyeball the fellow, that means, what I've got to do, I call my guy in DC, I pass along my tip, and I'm not even sure Nelson here isn't pulling my chain. What if Harbin *isn't* there? I don't keep a reputation with dud tips."

McWhitney said, "I don't give you dud tips. What's in it for me? He's right exactly where I told you."

"Have a good one, Nels."

"You too, Jack." McWhitney waved, then said to Parker, "About halfway between Cincinnati and Dayton, Interstate 75, they're putting in a new restaurant, rest area. There's a spot they're gonna blacktop for the parking lot very soon now but not yet, not till the structure's a little further along. A month ago, it was just messed-up fill in there, bulldozed a little, a lot of wide tire tracks. A few more weeks, they gotta lay that black-top before winter freezes the ground, but not yet."

"I hate it when somebody's plausible," Sandra said. "Everything fits together like Legos. Life doesn't do that."

"Every once in a while," McWhitney told her, "the plausible guy has the goods."

Parker said, "So McWhitney gave you the tip, and you gave it to somebody you know in DC—"

"In the US marshals' office."

"And they're sending somebody to check it out. If the body's there, you get your reward money. They're calling you here?"

"Not on the *bar's* phone," she said. "On my cell."

"All right."

"Pretty soon, they'll call," Sandra said. She did all her talking with her right hand in her coat pocket. "If they say Harbin's there, fine. If they say Mr. Harbin's still among the missing, I'm gonna feel very embarrassed."

"He's there," McWhitney said.

"But I'll get over my embarrassment," she told them, "because I'll still have a little something to give them, make up for the inconvenience. Originally, I just had Nelson here." She smiled around at them all. "But now," she said, "I got a twofer."

4

McWhitney said, "I'd better lock up."

He had to walk down to the end of the bar and open the flap there to come out, then walk back past the others on this side. Sandra stepped back against the line of booths so he wouldn't pass behind her, then said to Parker, "Funny you should happen by."

"Is it?"

"You find yourself in the neighborhood, just the same day Dalesia slips his bonds."

Returning to the others, staying now on this side of the bar, McWhitney said, "Sandra, don't excite yourself. We aren't helping Nick. He isn't gonna let us know where he is."

Skeptical, Sandra said, "Why? Because you'd turn him in?"

"That's the last thing we'd do," McWhitney said,

"and he knows it. Unless it was turn him in like you're turning in Harbin."

She shook her head. "You were a team."

"Not any more."

Parker said, "If they take him again, all he has for bargaining chips is the money and us."

"Well, it's me more than you," McWhitney said. "He knows this place here."

"I think," Claire said carefully, "he knows our phone number."

Sandra looked at her with a little smile. "You mean, he *knows* your phone number. He's used your phone number. Roy Keenan and me, we looked at that number. Nick Dalesia never did have a wide range of telephone pals. Ms. Willis stood out."

Claire shrugged. "I never actually met the man," she said. "I have no real link with him at all. I was looking for somebody to blacktop my driveway. I forget who said they'd have Mr. Dalesia call me. I talked to him twice, but I thought he sounded unreliable."

"That's nice," Sandra said. "As long as Nick isn't there to say it didn't happen that way."

"That's what we're saying," McWhitney told her. He had taken the stool next to Parker, with Claire beyond, the three facing Sandra with her right hand in her pocket and her back braced against the booth's tall coatrack.

"All right," Sandra said. "But while we're waiting

here, it might be we could do some other business together. I mean, if this Harbin thing turns out to be on the up-and-up."

McWhitney said, "What kind of business?"

"You people took a lot of money up there in New England," Sandra said, "but then you had to leave it. That's only three days ago, too soon for you to dare to go back." To Parker, she said, "But Dalesia might go for it, that's why you came here to see McWhitney. How to keep the money safe from your friend without exposing yourselves to the law."

Parker said, "I think Nick's pretty busy right about now."

"I think your Nick needs money bad right about now," Sandra said.

McWhitney said, "You aren't, I hope, gonna say we should tell you where it is, so you can go get it and bring it back to us."

Sandra's free left hand made a shrugging gesture. "Why not? One woman could get in there and out, and then you've got something instead of nothing."

"If you come back," McWhitney said.

Parker said, "We'll take our chances. If you *don't* get in and out, if they grab you with the money, they're gonna ask you who told you where it was. What reason would you have not to tell them?"

Sandra thought about that, then nodded. "I see how it could look," she said. "All right, it was just an offer."

McWhitney said, "I can't give you people meals in this place. How much longer you think we're gonna wait?"

"Until they call me," she said.

Parker said, "Call them."

Sandra didn't like that. "What for? They'll do what they're doing, and then they'll call me."

"You call them," Parker said. "You tell them, speed it up, your tipster's getting anxious, he's afraid there's a double-cross coming along."

"It won't do any good to push—" she said, and a small, flat, almost toneless brief ring sounded. "At last," she said, looking suddenly relieved, showing an anxiety of her own she'd been covering till now. Her right hand stayed in the coat pocket while her left dipped into the other pocket and came out with the cell phone. Her thumb clipped into the second ring and she said, "Keenan. Sure it's me, it's Roy's business phone. What have you got?"

Parker watched McWhitney. Was the man tensing? Had he given the bounty hunter the truth?

Suddenly Sandra beamed, the last of the tension gone, and her right hand came empty out of the pocket. "That's great. I thought my source was reliable, but you can never be sure. I'll come into the New York office tomorrow for the check? Fine, Wednesday. Oh, Roy's around here somewhere."

McWhitney looked very alert, but then relaxed

again as Sandra said into the phone, "My best to Linda. Thanks, she's fine. Talk to you later." She broke the connection, pocketed the phone, and said to McWhitney, "It worked out. He's who he is, he's where you said."

"Like I said." Now that it was over, McWhitney suddenly looked tired. "Let me throw you people out of here now."

As they walked down the bar toward the door, Sandra said, "You got any more goods like that stashed around, you know what I mean, goods with some value on them, give me a call."

"What I should have done," McWhitney said, as he unlocked the door to let them out, "I should have held out for a finder's fee."

Sandra laughed and walked away toward her car, and McWhitney shut the door. They could hear the click of the lock.

5

Claire's place was on a lake in north-central New Jersey, surrounded mostly by seasonal houses, only a fifth or so occupied year-round. In several of these houses were hollow walls, crawl spaces, unused attic stubs, where Parker kept his stashes.

Two days after the overnight trip to Long Island, he finally stashed the duffel bag he'd brought from upstate New York, then drove to put gas in Claire's Toyota, paying with cash from the duffel, money on which nobody had a record of the numbers. Heading back, he was about to turn in at Claire's driveway when he saw through the trees another car parked down in there, black or dark gray. Instead, then, he went on to the next driveway and steered in there, stopping at a house boarded up for the winter.

He probably knew this house better than the owners did, including the whereabouts of the key that most of the seasonal people hid near their front doors where workmen or anybody else could find them. He didn't need the key this time. He walked around the side of the house opposite Claire's place and on the lake side came to a wide porch that in summer was screened. Now the screens were stored in the space beneath the porch.

Parker moved past the porch and across a cleared lane between the buildings kept open for utility workers and on to the blindest corner of Claire's house. Moving along the lake side, not stepping up on the porch, he could see across and through a window at the interior. Claire was seated on the sofa in there, talking with two men seated in chairs angled toward her. He couldn't see the men clearly, but there was no tension in the room. Claire was speaking casually, gesturing, smiling.

Parker turned away and went back to the next-door house, where he stepped up onto the porch, took a seat in a wooden Adirondack armchair there, and waited.

Five minutes. Two men in dark topcoats and snap-brim hats came out of Claire's front door, and Claire stood in the doorway to speak to them. The men moved together, as though from habit rather than intention. With the hats, they looked like FBI agents from fifties movies, except that in the fifties movies one of them would not have been black.

The two men each touched a finger to the brim of

his hat. Claire said something else, easy and unconcerned, and shut the door as the men got into their anonymous pool car, the white driving, and went away.

Parker went back around this house to the Toyota, drove to Claire's place, and thumbed the visor control that opened the garage. When he stepped from the garage to the kitchen Claire was in there, making coffee. "Want some?"

"Yes. FBI?"

"Yes. I told them my blacktop story, and said I'd try to remember who gave me Mr. Dalesia's name, but it had been a while."

He sat at the kitchen table. "They bought it?"

"They bought the house, the lake, the attractive woman, the sunlight."

"They gave you their card, and that was it?"

"Probably," she said. "They said they might call me if they thought of anything else to ask, and I said I thought I might be going on an early-winter vacation soon, I wasn't sure." Bringing Parker's coffee to the table, she said, "Should I?"

"Yes. We'll go together."

Surprised, she sat across from him and said, "You have a place in mind?"

"When I was in Massachusetts last week," he said, "they were talking about something called leaf peeping."

Even more surprised, she said, "Leaf peeping? Oh, that's because the fall colors change on the trees."

"That's it."

"People go to New England just to see the colors on the trees." She considered. "They call them leaf peepers?"

"That's what I heard."

She looked out the kitchen window toward the lake. Most of the trees around here were evergreens, but there were some that changed color in the fall; down here, that wouldn't be for another month, and not as showy as New England. "It makes them sound silly," she said. "Leaf peepers. You make a whole trip to look at leaves. I guess it is silly, really."

"We wouldn't be the only ones there."

She looked at him. "What you really want to do," she said, "is be near the money."

"I want to know what's happening there. You have to drive and pay for the place we stay, because I don't have ID. And if I'm a leaf peeper, I'm not a bank robber."

"You're a leaf peeper if you're with me."

"That's right."

"On your own, nobody would buy you for a leaf peeper," she said, and smiled, and then stopped smiling.

Sensing a dark memory rising up inside her, he said, "Everything's all finished up there. It's done. Nothing's going to happen except we look at leaves and we look at a church."

"A church," she echoed.

Rising, he said, "Let me get a map, I'll show you the area we want. Then you can find a place up there—"

"A bed-and-breakfast."

"Right. We'll stay for a week." Nodding at the phone on the wall, he said, "Then you can make your answering machine message be that you're on vacation for a week, and you can give the place you're gonna be."

"Because," she said, "what's going to happen up there already happened."

"That's right," he said.

6

You folks here for the robbery?"

The place was called Bosky Rounds, and the pictures on the web site had made it look like somewhere that Hansel and Gretel might have stopped off. Deep eaves, creamy stucco walls, broad dark green wooden shutters flanking the old-fashioned multipaned windows, and a sun god knocker on the front door. The Bosky Rounds gimmick, though they wouldn't have used the word, was that they offered maps of nearby hiking trails through the forest, for those leaf peepers who would like to be surrounded by their subject. It was the most rustic and innocent accommodation Claire could find, and Parker had agreed it was perfect for their purposes.

And the first thing Mrs. Bartlett, the owner, the nice motherly lady in the frilled apron and the faint aroma of apple pie, said to them was, "You folks here for the robbery?"

"Robbery?" Claire managed to look both astonished and worried. "What robbery? You were robbed?"

"Oh, not *me*, dear," and Mrs. Bartlett offered a throaty chuckle and said, "It was all over the television. Not five miles from here, last week, a week ago tomorrow, a whole *gang* attacked the bank's armored cars with *bazookas*."

"Bazookas!" Claire put her hand to her throat, then leaned forward as though she suspected this nice old lady was pulling her leg. "Wouldn't that burn up all the money?"

"Don't ask me, dear, I just know they blew up everything, my cousin told me it was like a war movie."

"Was he *there*?"

"No, he rushed over as soon as he heard it on his radios." To Parker she said, "He has all these different kinds of radios, you know." Back to Claire she said, "You really haven't heard about it?"

"Oh, us New Yorkers," Claire said, with a laugh and a shrug. "We really are parochial, you know. If it doesn't happen in Central Park, we don't know a thing about it." Handing over her credit card, she said, "I tell you what. Let us check in and unpack, and then you'll tell us all about it."

"I'd be delighted," said Mrs. Bartlett. "And you're the Willises," she said, looking at the credit card.

"Claire and Henry," Claire said.

Mrs. Bartlett put the card in her apron pocket. "I put you in room three upstairs," she said. "It really is the nicest room in the house."

"Lovely."

"I'll give you back your card when you come down." She turned to say to Parker, "And you'll have tea?"

"Sure. Thanks."

It was a large room, with two large bright many-paned windows, frills on every piece of furniture, and a ragged old Oriental carpet. They unpacked into the old tall dresser and the armoire, there being no closet, and Parker went over to look out the window toward the rear of the house. The trees began right there, red and yellow and orange and green. "I'll have to look on the map," he said. "See where this is."

"You mean, from the robbery site," Claire said, and laughed. "Don't worry, Mrs. Bartlett will tell you, in detail. Will you mind sitting through that?"

"It's a good idea," Parker said, "for me to know what the locals think happened."

"Fine. But one thing."

He looked at her. "Yeah?"

"If she gets a part wrong," Claire said, "don't correct her."

*   *   *

Over tea and butter cookies in the communal parlor downstairs, Mrs. Bartlett gave them an exhaustive and mostly accurate description of what had gone on up in those woods last Friday night. It turned out, she said, that two of the local banks were going to combine, so all of the money from one was going to the other. It was all very hush-hush and top secret and nobody was supposed to know anything about it, but it turned out *somebody* knew what was going on, because, just at this intersection here—she showed them on the county map—where these two small roads meet, nobody knows how many gangsters suddenly appeared with bazookas, and smashed up all the armored cars— there were four armored cars, with all the bank's papers and everything in addition to the money—and drove off with the one armored car with the money in it, and when the police found the armored car later all the money was gone.

Parker said, "How did the gangsters know which armored car had the money in it?"

"Well, *that*," Mrs. Bartlett told them, leaning close to confide a secret, "that was where the scandal came in. The wife of the bank owner, Mrs. Langen, she was in cahoots with the robbers!"

Claire said, "In cahoots? The banker's wife? Oh, Mrs. Bartlett."

"No, it's true," Mrs. Bartlett promised them. "It seems she'd taken up with a disgraced ex-guard in her husband's bank. He went to jail for stealing something or other, and when he came back they started right up again where they left off, and the first thing you know they robbed her own husband's bank!"

"But the law got them," Parker suggested.

"Oh, yes, of course, the police immediately captured *them*," Mrs. Bartlett said. "They'll pay for their crimes, don't you worry. But not the robbers, no, not the people who actually took the money."

"The people with the bazookas," Parker said, because the Carl-Gustaf antitank weapons from Sweden had not been bazookas.

"Those people," Mrs. Bartlett agreed. "And the money, too, of course. There've been police and state troopers and FBI men and I don't know what all around here all week. I even had three state police investigators staying here until Tuesday."

"I'm sorry we missed them," Claire murmured.

"Oh, they were just like anybody," Mrs. Bartlett said. "You wouldn't know anything to look at them."

"I suppose," Claire said, turning to Parker, "we ought to go see where this robbery took place."

"It's *still* traffic jams over there," Mrs. Bartlett said. "People going, and stopping, and taking pictures, though I have no idea what they think they're taking pictures of. Just some burned trees, that's all."

"It's the excitement," Claire suggested. "People want to be around the excitement."

"Well, if you're going over there," Mrs. Bartlett said, "the best time is in the morning. Before nine o'clock." She leaned forward again for another confidence. "Tourists, generally, are very slugabed," she told them.

"Well," Claire said, "they are on vacation."

Parker said, "So, when we go out to dinner, we shouldn't go in that direction."

"Oh, no. There are some lovely places . . . Let me show you."

There was a specific route Parker wanted, but he needed Mrs. Bartlett to suggest it. He found reasons not to be enthusiastic about her first three dinner suggestions, but the fourth would be on a route that would take them right past the church. "New England seafood," he said. "That sounds fine. You want to give Claire the directions?"

"I'd be very happy to."

7

It was still a couple of hours before sunset, and Claire wanted to walk outside a while, to work off the stiffness of the long car ride. They stepped out the front door, and a young guy was just bouncing up onto the porch. "Hi," he said, and they nodded and would have passed him but he stopped, frowned, pointed at them, and said, "I didn't talk with you folks, did I?"

"No," Claire said.

"Well, let me—" He was patting himself all over, frisking himself for something, while he talked, a kind of distracted smile on his face. He looked to be in his early twenties, with thick windblown brown hair, a round expectant face, and large black-framed glasses that made him look like an owl. A friendly owl. He wore a dark gray car coat with a cell phone dangling in front of it from a black leather strap around his neck, and jeans and boots, and it was the car coat he searched as he said, "I'm not a nut or anything, I wanna show you my bona fides, I've got my card here somewh— Oh, here it is." And from an interior pocket he plucked a business card, which he handed to Claire.

The card was pale yellow, with maroon letters centered, reading

TERRY MULCANY
Journalist

laureled with phone, fax and cell phone numbers, plus an e-mail address. There was no terrestrial address.

Claire said, "It doesn't say who you're a journalist for."

"I'm freelance," Mulcany said, smiling nervously, apparently not sure they'd be impressed by his status. "I specialize in true crime. No, keep it," he said, as Claire was about to hand the card back. "I've got boxes of them." The grin semaphored and he said, "I lose them all the time, and then I find them."

"That's nice," Claire said. "Excuse me, we were just—"

"Oh, no, I don't want to take up your time," Mulcany said. "I just— You heard about the robbery, here last week."

"Mrs. Bartlett just told us all about it."

"Oh, is that her name, the lady here?"

Claire bent to him. "You aren't staying here?"

"Oh, no, I can't afford this place," and the smile flickered some more. "Not until my advance comes in. I've got a deal with Spotlight to do a book on the robbery, so I'm just here getting the background, taking some pictures."

"Well, I'm sorry, we can't help," Claire told him. "We just heard about the robbery ourselves half an hour ago."

"That's fine, I don't expect—" Mulcany interrupted himself a lot, now saying, "You're here for the foliage, aren't you?"

Claire nodded. "Of course."

"So you'll be out, driving around, walking around," Mulcany said. "If you see anything, anything at all, anything that seems a little weird, out of the ordinary, let me know. Call me on my cell," he said, holding it up for them to look at. "If you find me something and I use it," he said, grinning in full, letting the cell phone drop to his coat front again, "I'll give you the credit, and I'll put you in the index!"

"Well, I don't know what we might see," Claire told him, "but that's a tempting offer. I'll keep your card."

"Great." He was suddenly in a hurry to move on. "And I gotta check a couple details with— What was her name again?"

"Mrs. Bartlett. Like the pear."

"Oh, great," Mulcany said. "That I can remember. Thanks a lot!" And he hurried into Bosky Rounds.

Claire laughed as she and Parker started away from the B and B and down the town road with its wide dirt strip instead of a sidewalk. "Isn't that nice?" she said. "You lost money on that expedition, but he's going to make some. So it's working out for somebody, after all."

"I don't like him being here," Parker said.

"Oh, he's harmless," she said.

Parker shook his head. "On some wall," he said, "that guy's got those wanted posters tacked up. This time, he looked at you. Next time, maybe he looks at me."

8

As they drove toward their New England seafood dinner, Parker said, "Nick's the one found the church. It's abandoned for years, off on a side road. The original idea was, we'd spend the first night there, split up the cash, head out in the morning. But the law presence was so intense we couldn't move, and we couldn't take the cash with us. So we left it there."

"In the church."

"We'll be going by it in a few minutes."

"I won't see much in the dark."

"I don't want you to even slow down," Parker told her. "The story the law is giving out is that Nick escaped before he could tell them anything, but they don't always tell the truth, you know."

"You think they might know the money's there, in the church?"

"And they might have it staked out, waiting for us to

come back. So we'll just drive by. In daylight, I'll try to get a better look at it."

They kept driving, on dark, small, thinly populated roads, until he said, "It's on the right."

A small white church crouched in darkness, with parking around it. Claire looked at it as she drove by and said, "I don't see anybody."

"You wouldn't."

They passed the church again on their way back from the not-bad seafood dinner, and still didn't see any sign of anybody in or near the place. But then they walked into Bosky Rounds and there in the communal parlor they did see somebody they knew: Susan Loscalzo.

She got to her feet with a big smile when they walked in, tossing *Yankee* magazine back onto the coffee table as she said, "Well, hello, you two. Fancy running into you guys here."

9

There were five guest rooms at Bosky Rounds, and with Sandra's arrival late this afternoon all five were occupied. Now, in another corner of the communal parlor, two couples murmured together, planning their itinerary for tomorrow. Glancing toward them, ignoring the fact that Parker and Claire hadn't said anything to her greeting, Sandra said, "I saw a bar on the way here looking like it had possibilities. Want to check it out?"

"Sure," Parker said, and to Claire he said, "You want to come along?"

"Absolutely."

Nodding, with a little smile at Claire, Sandra said, "One car or two?"

"We'll follow you," Parker said.

As they turned toward the front door, Sandra looked around and said, "Where's Mrs. Muskrat?"

Claire said, "I think we're on our own till morning."

"It's the kind of place," Sandra said, "I feel I oughta check in with the proctor before I do anything."

Her car, in the gravel lot beside the building, was a small black Honda Accord that would have been anonymous if it weren't for the two whip antennas arcing high over its top, making it look like some outsized tropical insect in the wrong weather zone. Sandra got behind the wheel with a wave, and Claire started the Toyota to follow.

Driving down the dark road with that humped black insect in front of her, Claire said, "Tell me about Sandra. Does she have a guy?"

"She isn't straight," Parker said. "She lives with a woman on Cape Cod, and the woman has a child. Sandra supports the child. She thought she was the brains behind Roy Keenan and maybe she was. We got linked to her because she wanted the Harbin reward money and we led her to it. What she wants now I don't know."

"The bank money?"

"Maybe." Parker shook his head, not liking it. "It's not in her line," he said. "I'd think she'd be out looking for another Roy Keenan now. I don't know what she's doing."

"Was Roy Keenan straight?"

"Oh, yeah. That was just a business arrangement. She'd be out of sight with the handgun while Keenan asked the questions."

Claire said, "I don't mean to be a matchmaker, but why wouldn't McWhitney be a good new Roy?"

"Because he's too hotheaded and she's too hard," Parker said. "One of them would kill the other in a month, I don't know which. This looks like the place."

It was. The Honda, antennae waving, turned in at an old-fashioned sprawling roadhouse with a fairly full parking lot to one side. The main building, two stories high, was flanked by wide enclosed porches, brightly lit, while the second floor was completely dark. A large floodlit sign out by the road, at right angles to the parking lot, told drivers from both directions WAY-WARD INN.

They parked the cars next to one another and met on the gravel. "I didn't go inside the place before," Sandra said. "It seemed to me, big enough for some privacy, dining rooms on both sides, bar in the middle."

"Bar," Claire said.

"You're my kind of girl," Sandra told her, and led the way as Claire lifted an eyebrow at Parker.

The entrance was a wide doorway centered in the front of the building, at the end of a slate path from the parking area. Sandra pushed in first, the others following, and inside was a wide dark-carpeted hall with a maître d's lectern prominent. To left and right, wide doorways showed the bright dining rooms in the enclosed porches, the customers now thinning out toward the end of the day. Behind the lectern a broad dark staircase led upward, and next to that a dimly lit hall extended back to what could be seen was a low-lit bar. Atop the lectern a cardboard sign read PLEASE SEAT YOURSELF.

"That's us," Sandra said, and led the way past the lectern and down the hall to the bar, which was more full at this hour than the dining rooms, but also quieter, with lower lighting. The room was broad, with the bar along the rear, high-backed booths on both sides, and black Formica-top tables filling the center.

Sandra pointed toward a booth on the left: "That looks pretty alone."

"Good," Parker said.

They went over there, Sandra sitting to face the front entrance, Claire opposite her, Parker beside Claire. From where he sat, the bar's mirrored back wall gave him a good view of the hall down toward the entrance.

A young waitress in black appeared almost immediately, hugging tall black menus to her breast. "Supper menu?"

"We ate," Claire said. "Just drinks."

"I might as well look at it," Sandra said.

Claire and Parker both ordered scotch on the rocks while Sandra decided on the popcorn shrimp and a glass of red wine. When the waitress went away, Sandra explained, "I didn't really have dinner, I just drove up."

"You were in a hurry," Parker told her.

Sandra gave him a frank look. "I wasn't out to make trouble for you boys last time," she said, "and I'm not now. But now the situation is different than it was."

"Keenan's dead," Parker suggested.

"And my government," Sandra said, "is jerking me around."

Parker said, "They want your source?"

"Absolutely not. That isn't the way it works." To Claire she said, "Sometimes the government needs information. The deal is, if you've got that information and you're a legitimate licensed investigator, and you give them that information, or you sell it to them, they don't turn around and use it against *you*. It's kind of immunity plus a paycheck."

"Not bad," Claire said.

Parker said, "So what went wrong?"

"Harbin was too popular," Sandra said, and the waitress arrived with their orders. "I gotta eat just a minute," Sandra said.

She was hungry. She scarfed down a couple large mouthfuls of popcorn shrimp, with a swig of red wine as though it were beer, and Parker looked at the other customers in this room.

Tourists. Nobody that looked like a local, only visitors not ready for this day to end. Conversations were low and easy, but here and there punctuated by a yawn. Nobody looked like law.

Sandra waved at the waitress, then called to her, "Same again," and said to Parker, "Three different agencies had money out on Harbin, and a fourth had a leash on him, and none of them knew anything about any of the others. So right now they gotta sort that out so they can decide, when they pay *me*, which agency budget does it come out of. Right now, they're fighting about it."

"They're fighting about which of them has to pay you."

"That's about it." Sandra shrugged, and now she sipped a little wine. "In the meantime, you know I've got expenses."

"I know," Parker said.

"Roy took too long on the Harbin thing," Sandra said. "That's why he got careless at the end there. He figured, no penny-ante punk could *really* just disappear like that. So we were pretty much running on empty when I finally got my answer to the question, and the bitch of it is, I'm *still* running on empty until they get their official heads out of their official asses."

"That's too bad," Parker said.

"Meaning," Sandra said, "why should you give a shit. The only other two places for cash money I know of right now, to tide me over, is your bank score and Mr. Nicholas Dalesia."

Parker said, "Dalesia?"

"You don't think there's reward money out on him,

right now?" Sandra asked. "And only one agency, no waiting."

"I don't know where he is," Parker said. "I told you that."

"You did, and I believe you, and I believe if you found out where he was he wouldn't live long because he's a lot more dangerous to you than I am or anybody else."

"Maybe."

The waitress brought Sandra's seconds and she ate a while more, then said, "You know Dalesia isn't ten miles from here right this minute."

"Probably."

"He's got no money, no ID, no transportation. Does he have anybody around here he can go to?"

"Not that I know of."

Sandra considered. "Maybe a shut-in, take over a house for a few days."

Parker said, "Even shut-ins get visitors, phone calls. Medicine delivered."

"Well, he's a bad penny, he'll show up." Sandra used the paper napkin on her lips and said, "The point is, you see where I am."

"In my face," Parker said.

"Sorry about that," Sandra said. "I need cash, and this is where it is, or where it's gonna be. You know I've got dossiers on you and your partners."

"That your lady friend is holding, out there on Cape Cod."

"Well, she's gone visiting," Sandra said.

Parker nodded. "Is that right."

"Maybe with family, maybe with friends. Maybe here, maybe there. She's hoping she'll hear from me pretty soon."

Claire said, "Sandra, you seem like a smart person."

"Thank you," Sandra said, and gave Claire a cool look with not much question in it.

"Which means," Claire said, "you already know what you want out of this talk here."

"Sure," Sandra said, and shrugged. "A partnership." She switched the cool look to Parker. "Think of me as the successor firm to Nick Dalesia," she said.

Parker said, "You want his share?"

"I don't deserve his share," Sandra said, "because I wasn't around for the first part. But I deserve half of his share, and you and McWhitney split the other half." Waving toward the waitress again, giving her the check-signing signal, she said, "We're just doing a little business here, so I'll pick up the tab. You don't have to agree or say anything. I'm in, that's all. It's not your fault, and it's not mine, and we'll learn to live with it. And you'll find I have my uses. In the meantime, we'll all be cosy together, over at— What do they call that place?"

"The waiting room," Claire said.

10

Following Sandra out the front door of Wayward Inn, Parker said quietly, "Let her go first."

"All right."

They said good night, said they'd see one another tomorrow, and got into the cars. It took Claire a while to decide the best place to put her handbag, and by then Sandra had backed out, spun around, and headed for the exit.

As they followed, Parker said, "Hang back. She won't let you disappear out of her mirrors, but she'll let you hang back."

"You aren't going to do anything to her, are you?"

"I can't. When she and her partner Keenan were first looking for Harbin, they made dossiers of what they could find out about the people at that meeting where he disappeared. Nelson's bar, Nick phoning you.

If something happens to Sandra, her friend on Cape Cod gives that stuff to the law."

"They already know my phone number."

"Getting it again, from a second direction, means they'll take a closer look. You don't want that."

Claire shook her head, eyes on the taillights out in front of her. "If I have to give up my house, I will," she said. "Be Claire somebody else, I will. But I won't want to."

"We're trying to make it not happen," Parker said. "Right now, Sandra's on guard, something could kick her off. Her friend I don't know anything about. But so far, we can deal with it. The worst would be if McWhitney found out she was here."

"Why?"

"He'd kill her, right away, first, worry about dossiers later. Then everybody has to move."

Claire brooded about that. "Do you think he'll come up?"

"Not now, not over the weekend, he's still got that bar to run. Early next week, he might. Up ahead there, at the intersection, you're gonna turn left. There's a deli on the right, parking lot beyond it. Make the turn, go in there, shut everything down."

Claire nodded and said, "I thought maybe we weren't going straight back."

The intersection ahead was topped by a yellow blinker signal. Sandra's Honda drove under it and through. Claire, without a signal, made the left, made a right U-turn into the deli's parking lot, tucked the Toyota in next to a Dumpster back there, and switched everything off. They waited, and then a black car went by out there, from left to right, accelerating.

Parker said, "Give her a minute, then go back out and go straight through the intersection."

"All right," she said. "Where are we going?"

"To visit the money," Parker said. "Start now," and she did. As they jounced out onto the road, he said, "We don't wanna do all this dance and the money's long gone."

"Stop at the road up there on the right. Then just drive around a while. Give me half an hour."

"All right," she said, and when she stopped at the corner, the two visible houses both dark for the night, she said, "Will you bring some out?"

"No," he said. "We don't want samples. We just want to know it's there. And alone."

He got out of the Toyota and walked down the dark side road. There was partial cloud cover above, but some starlight got through, enough to see the difference between the blacktop and the shoulder.

It was not quite midnight now, a Thursday in October, nothing happening on this secondary road at all, no lights in the occasional dwelling he walked past. Soon, ahead of him on the right, he could make out the white hulk of the church. It was a small white clapboard structure with a wooden steeple. Across the road, difficult to see at night, was a narrow two-story white clapboard house that must have been connected to the church. Both buildings had been empty a long time.

Parker started with the house first. If there were a law presence here, watching the place, this would be the most comfortable spot to wait in.

But the house was empty, and when he crossed the road, so was the church. There was no sign that anybody had been in it since he and Dalesia and McWhitney had quit it a week ago.

Finally, he went up to the choir loft to check on the money. The bank had been transporting its cash in standard white rectangular packing boxes, and the church had stored its missals and hymnals up in the choir loft in the same way; not identical boxes, but similar. Parker and McWhitney and Dalesia had mixed the bank's boxes in with the church's boxes and left them there, arranging them so that, if anybody came upstairs and started looking in these boxes, the first three would contain books.

They still did. And the ones behind and beneath them still contained the close-packed stacks of green. Nothing had changed. The money still waited for them.

*　　*　　*

When they got back to Bosky Rounds, someone was seated in the dark on the porch, in a rocking chair. Rocking forward into the light, Sandra said, "Visiting our money?"

"Your part is still there," Parker told her.

11

Breakfast at Bosky Rounds was in a room smaller than the communal parlor, an oblong crammed with square tables for two, at the right front corner of the building, with a view mostly of the road out front. Friday morning, Parker and Claire ate a late breakfast, each with a different part of the *New York Times*, Parker facing the doorway through which the entrance foyer and Mrs. Bartlett's desk could be seen.

The small bell over the entrance tinkled and a woman appeared, stopping in front of Mrs. Bartlett's desk, her profile to Parker. She was a good-looking blonde in her twenties, tall, slim in a tan deerskin coat over chocolate-colored slacks and black boots, with a heavy black shoulder bag hanging to her left hip. Parker knew her, and she would know him, too. Her name was Detective Second Grade Gwen Reversa.

Quietly, Parker said, "Lift your paper. Read it that way."

She did so, her expressionless face and the room behind her disappearing behind the newsprint. Out there, Mrs. Bartlett and Detective Reversa talked, pals, greeting one another, discussing something. Parker couldn't quite hear what they were saying, and then the bell tinkled again, and when he said, "All right," and Claire lowered the paper, only Mrs. Bartlett was there.

Claire said, "Can I look?"

"She's gone."

Claire looked anyway, then said, "She's a cop."

"State, plainclothes. You could hear what they were saying."

Claire shrugged. "She was just checking in. Wanted to know if Mrs. Bartlett had seen anything interesting since last time they talked." Without irony she said, "The answer was no."

"Good."

"But she'd recognize you?"

"She made a traffic stop on me, before the job. She's the reason you had to report the Lexus stolen and get this rental."

"I liked the Lexus," Claire said.

"You wouldn't have."

"Oh, I know." Claire looked around again at the

space where the detective had been. "But she was *here*."

"She's part of the search," Parker said. "She was on that heist from the beginning. She and a bunch more are still around because they know Nick's got to be somewhere around here and the money's got to be somewhere around here."

"You can't stay here," Claire said. "Not if she knows what you look like."

"I know," he said. "We've got to get this over with."

There was a low flower-pattern settee in the corner of Mrs. Bartlett's office, and Sandra Loscalzo was seated on it, looking at local maps and brochures from a display rack mounted on the wall. Mrs. Bartlett was at her desk doing puzzles in a crossword book, and Parker stopped to say to her, "We wondered if you could give us some advice."

"If I can," she said, putting down her pencil.

"We thought," he said, "we'd like to look at the countryside from a height somewhere that we could get a sense of the whole area."

"Oh, I know just the place," Mrs. Bartlett said, and took one of the maps from the display rack near Sandra, who did not look up from her own researches. "It was a Revolutionary War battle site. Just wonderful views. Rutledge Ridge."

With a red pen, she drew the route on the map,

naming off the roads as she went. They thanked her and took the map out to the Toyota.

Sandra drove up to the lookout five minutes after they arrived. Seemingly unbroken forest fell away on three sides in clumps and clusters of bright color, rising only in the north. A few other tourists were up here, but the parking and observation area was large enough for everybody to have as much privacy as they wanted.

Sandra got out of the Honda and came over to the low stone wall that girdled the view, Claire seated on the wall, Parker standing next to her. "You know that cop," she said, as a greeting.

"She knows me," Parker said.

"I get that." To Claire, Sandra said, "Very smooth, with the newspaper."

"*You* noticed."

"Well, I take an interest." To Parker, she said, "You looked the place over last night. Can we go and get it? How much longer do we wait?"

"I don't want to wait at all, with that detective around," Parker told her. "But if she's still here, that means we've still got a lot of law to deal with. The law is looking for a lot of heavy boxes of cash. You rent a truck around here right now, somebody's gonna stop you just to see who you are."

"What about three or four cars? You, me, Claire, and McWhitney."

"Four strangers, all going off the tourist trails, getting together, making a little convoy."

Sandra frowned out at the view, not seeming to see it. "If I knew where this goddamn stash was—"

"In a church," he said.

She looked at him, wanting to be sure he was serious. "A church?"

Nick Dalesia found it. Long time abandoned. Water and electricity switched off but still there. The idea was to just hole up overnight, but the heat was too intense, we had to leave the cash behind."

"In boxes."

"Up in the choir loft. Already church boxes up there, hymns and things."

"That's nice." Sandra paced, rubbing the knuckles of her right hand into her left palm. "I know you don't want to tell me where this church is, not yet, but that's okay. The time comes, we'll go there together."

"That's right," Parker said.

"Unless," Claire said, "you just can't stay here any more."

"Well, he can't stay here any more," Sandra said.

"If I go away and come back when the law is gone," Parker said, "a lot of things can happen."

Sandra paced, rubbing those knuckles, then stopped to say, "I tell you what. You and me, we drive down to Long Island, six, seven hours, we talk it over with McWhitney."

Parker looked at her. "You want to see McWhitney?"

Sandra shrugged. "Don't worry, I'm no Roy Keenan, I won't turn my back on him. But we'll tell him, you and me, we got an understanding, right?"

"Half of Nick."

"We'll go now," Sandra said. "Get there in daylight. Claire can hold the fort, let Mrs. Muskrat know we're coming back. Right?"

"Sure," Claire said. "But why do you want to do the driving?"

"Because you are," Sandra told her. "And you are because he isn't sure his license would play nice with cop computers. Me, I'm so clean they give me a gold medal every time they see me." She cocked a brow at Parker. "Ready?"

Parker looked at his watch. Nearly ten. He said to Claire, "I'll be back late tonight."

She nodded. "I'll be here."

12

Sandra was not so much a speeder as permanently aggressive, taking what small openings the road and the traffic gave her. It wasn't yet three-thirty in the afternoon when she parked diagonally across the street from McWhitney's bar, named in neon in the front window McW. "Surprise," she said, and gave Parker a twisted smile.

"Not too many surprises," Parker said.

Three-thirty on a Friday afternoon McW was a lot livelier than last time, about half full but with the clear sense that a greater crowd was on its way. McWhitney had a second bartender working, though he didn't really need him quite yet. McWhitney was busy, eyes and hands in constant motion, but he saw Parker and Sandra come in and immediately turned away, saying something to his assistant. Stripping off his apron, walking away, he pointed leftward at an empty booth and came down around the bar to join them at it.

"The lion lies down with the lamb," he said, not smiling.

Sandra grinned at him. "Which is which?"

"You got your Harbin," McWhitney told her, not hiding his dislike. "We got no more specials."

Sandra turned to Parker. "Tell him."

"She's in on the church with us," Parker said. "For half of Nick."

"In on the *church*?" McWhitney was offended. "She's *been* there?"

"Don't know where it is," Sandra said. "He won't tell me. But I think I can help you get the money out."

McWhitney frowned at Parker. "I don't like this."

"It isn't what any of us had in mind," Parker agreed. "But that neighborhood up there is still a hornet's nest, and the hornets are still out."

"There's a cop up there can make him," Sandra said, "And almost did."

McWhitney looked at Parker. "The woman cop?"

"Her."

McWhitney leaned back as his assistant bartender brought three beers, then left without a word. Taking a short sip, McWhitney said, "So we all just gotta go away for a while."

"Until what?" Parker asked him. "Until they get Nick again? Until Nick gets in there on his own and cleans it out? Until some kids fool around in there one night and find it?"

McWhitney nodded, but pointed a thumb at Sandra. "So what's she doing in it? She just happens to be this place, that place, and every time we see her we give her money? Half of Nick? What if Nick shows up?"

"You'll kill him," Sandra said.

McWhitney shook his head. "I still don't see what you're doing in here."

"I'll help dig," Sandra said, and nodded at the floor. "Probably in that basement of yours."

"Never mind my basement."

"Also," Sandra said, "I have a way to get your money."

Parker said, "You didn't say that before."

"I wanted to see how this meeting was gonna go, do I want to go through the trouble, or just screw you people and score it on my own."

"Listen to this," McWhitney said.

Parker said, "You've figured out a way to get the money out."

"I think so." To McWhitney she said, "You pretty well know the business operations around this neighborhood."

"Pretty well."

"Do you know a used-car lot, maybe kind of grungy, no cream puffs?"

McWhitney grinned for the first time since he'd laid

eyes on Sandra. "I know a dozen of them," he said. "Whadayou need?"

"A truck. A small beat-up old truck, delivery van, something like that. Black would be best, just so it isn't too shiny."

"A truck." McWhitney sounded disgusted. "To move the stash."

"That's right."

"What makes this truck wonderful? It's invisible?"

"Pretty much so," she said. "Whatever color it is, and I really would like black, we use the same color to paint out whatever name might already be on it. Then, on both doors, in white, we paint Holy Redeemer Choir."

"Holy shit," McWhitney said.

"We're the redeemers," Sandra told him. "It's okay if the name on the doors is a little amateurish, but we should try to do our best with it."

McWhitney slowly nodded. "The choir's coming to get their hymnals."

"And we'll *get* some, too," Sandra said, "in case anybody wants to look in back."

"Jesus, you always gotta insult me," McWhitney said. "Here I was thinking you weren't so bad."

"I was used to dealing with Roy," she said, and shrugged.

Now McWhitney laughed out loud. "You should thank me for breaking up the partnership."

Parker said, "Can you get this truck? Fix it up about the name?"

"It's gotta be me, doesn't it," McWhitney said. He didn't sound happy.

"You've got the legal front," Sandra said, and gestured at the bar around them. "This needs to be a truck with clean title, because you *will* be stopped, once you get up in that area."

Parker said, "Can you do all that this afternoon, or do we have to wait till Monday?"

"If I start now and find it in the next hour," McWhitney said, "the dealer can still deal with Motor Vehicles today, and I can come up there tomorrow. Maybe with dealer plates, but all the paperwork."

Taking out a business card, Sandra wrote the Bosky Rounds name and phone number on the back. As she pushed it across the table, she said, "Call us when you get there, we'll go out to the place together. I'm looking forward to see this truck you get."

"What you're looking forward to," McWhitney told her, "is what's in that church."

Sandra smiled. "Answered prayers," she said.

13

Parker drove the first half of the trip back, because his ID wasn't likely to be an issue before they got to the search zone. They stopped for dinner midway, at a chain restaurant along the road, where no locals would look at them and remember them. While they waited for their food, Parker said, "This whole thing is the wrong side of the street for you."

Sandra grimaced. "I don't think of it like that," she said. "What I think, there's no sides to the street because there is no street."

"What is there?"

She studied him, trying to decide how much to tell him, moving her fork back and forth on the table with her left hand. Then she shrugged, and left the fork alone, and said, "I figured it out when I was a little girl, what my idea of the world is."

"What's that?"

"A frozen lake," she said. "Bigger than you can see the end of. Every day, I get up, I gotta move a little more along the lake. I gotta be very careful and very wary, because I don't know where the ice is too thin. I gotta listen and watch."

"I've seen you do it."

She grinned and nodded, as though more pleased with him than with herself. "Yeah, you have."

They were both silent a minute, and then their food came. The waitress went away and Sandra picked up her fork, but then she paused to say, "You go see a war movie, the guy gets hurt, he yells 'Medic!', they come take him away, fix him up. Out here, you get hurt, you yell 'Medic!', you know what happens?"

"Yeah, I do."

"There's no sides," she said. "No street. We just do what we've got to do to get across the lake."

14

They got back to Bosky Rounds a little before nine that night. As Sandra pulled into a parking space beside the building, Claire came down off the porch, shaking her hand at them not to get out of the car. They waited, saying nothing, and she came over to slide into the backseat and say, "We have to leave."

He twisted half around in the seat to look at her, shadowed back there, far from the light on the porch. "Why?"

"That woman detective was here again," Claire said. "I heard her talking to Mrs. Bartlett. Because they haven't found Nick Dalesia, they're convinced all three of the robbers came back here, to get their money."

Parker said, "Why would they have an idea like that?"

"Because," Claire said, "they don't believe Nick could

hide this long without help, and who else would there be to help him?"

Sandra said, "I'd figure it that way, too."

"Nick's running a string of luck," Parker said. "For him. Not good for the rest of us."

"She brought wanted posters," Claire said. "Pictures of Nick, but drawings of the other two."

"I've seen them," Parker said. "They're not close enough."

"Not if you're just walking by," Claire told him. "But if you're sitting in that place having breakfast, and out in the office on the wall there's a drawing of you, people will make the connection."

Parker said, "She put posters on the wall?"

"They're papering the whole area, every public space." Claire leaned forward to put her elbow on the seatback and say, "I packed all of our things. Everything's in the car. I've just been waiting here for you to get back and then we can leave."

"No," he said.

"You can't stay," she insisted.

"But not that way," Parker said. "They've got your name, they've got your address, they've got your credit cards. You stay here tonight, tomorrow morning you check out. If you leave here tonight, you're just pointing an arrow at yourself."

Claire didn't like that. "What are *you* going to do?"

"McWhitney's coming up tomorrow with a truck,

we're gonna take that cash out of there. You've got my stuff in the car?"

"Yes."

"We'll move it over to this car. You go back to the room until tomorrow. I'll show Sandra where the church is and I'll stay there tonight." To Sandra he said, "When McWhitney gets here, you can lead him to the church."

Sandra said, "That probably won't be until tomorrow afternoon."

"When you come to the church," Parker told her, "bring me a coffee and Danish."

Claire said, "Then how will you get home?"

"I'll find a way," he said.

15

There won't be any twenty-four-hour delis around here," Sandra said.

"That's all right," Parker said. "I won't starve to death between now and tomorrow afternoon. Take the right at that yellow blinker up there."

"The right," she said, with some sort of edge, and looked sidelong at him. "That's where you lost me last night."

"Thought I lost you."

Now she laughed and made the right, and said, "McWhitney's sore because McWhitney's a sorehead. You know better."

"We'll see how it plays out."

"Don't fool around," she said. "We've got a deal."

"I know that."

"It's better for you. It's better for you and McWhitney both."

"You mean," Parker said, "we get our own pieces, and part of Nick."

"You get more than you were going to get," she said, "and now you're partners with somebody who can help you get it."

"Don't sell me any more," Parker said. "I get the idea."

"Sorry," she said.

He said, "I know, you were used to Keenan."

"I'm getting over it."

Till now there'd been no other traffic along this road, but a wavering oncoming light turned out to be a pickup truck, moving slowly and unsteadily, tacking rather than driving, with a driver fighting sleep. Sandra pulled far to the right to let him by, then looked in the rearview mirror and said, "The funny thing is, most fools get away with being fools."

"Until they count on it," Parker said. "There's a left turn coming up. Do you have a blanket or something in the trunk?"

"I keep a mover's pad back there," she said. "It's quilted, so I guess it's warm, but it's kind of stiff."

"Doesn't matter. We're coming up on the church now. I don't want you to stop. Church on the right, house on the left, both white. See?"

"Very remote," she said, as they drove on by.

"One of Nick's better ideas," Parker said. "Will you be able to find it tomorrow?"

"Oh, sure." She laughed. "I can usually find money."

"Up ahead here," he said, "there's a little bridge over a stream. The road curves down to the right to the bridge, and just before it there's a parking area on the right."

"For fishermen," she suggested.

"Probably. Stop there, and I'll get out and take the blanket and walk back. And do you have a bottle of water?"

"Right under your elbow there."

The road curved down and to the right, and ahead the old iron latticework of the bridge drew pale lines against the black. Sandra stopped the Honda. "See you sometime tomorrow."

"Right." Carrying the bottled water, he got out of the car and opened the trunk to pull the stiff pad out. He shut the trunk, rapped his knuckles on it once, and she drove away, over the bridge, taking all the light with her.

It would take a minute to adjust his eyes to the night. While waiting, he did his best to fold the blanket-size quilted pad into something he could carry. Finally, the simplest way was over his shoulders, like a cloak, which made him look more like a Plains Indian than anything else. But it was warm and not awkward, and easy to walk with.

Twice on the way back he saw headlights at a distance and stepped off the road till they went by, once into some woods and the other time along a one-lane dirt road meandering uphill.

And then, there ahead of him, were the two small pale buildings in the dark. Both were empty, but the house might be warmer and just a bit more comfortable, without the church's high ceilings. He went there and let himself in and decided on the smaller of the bedrooms upstairs.

It had been a long day; he spread the moving pad on the floor, rolled himself in it, and was soon asleep, and when he woke muddy daylight seeped through the room's one window. He was stiff, and not really rested, but he got up and drank some of the water, then went outside to relieve himself. While he was out there, he went over to look at the church again, and nothing had changed.

It was a long empty day. For part of it he walked, indoors or out, and other parts he sat against a wall in the empty house or curled into the moving pad again and slept. He woke from one of those with the long diagonals of late afternoon light coming in the window and Nick Dalesia seated cross-legged on the floor against the opposite wall. The revolver in his right hand, not exactly pointing anywhere, would belong to the dead marshal.

Parker sat up. "So there you are," he said.

16

"Where's your car?" Nick sounded strained, jumpy, a man without time for conversation.

That's the reason I'm alive, Parker thought. He came across me here, he would have killed me, but he needs wheels and he couldn't find the ones that brought me here. "Don't have one," he said.

Nick was all exposed nerve endings. Any answer might make him start shooting, just to do something. Twisting his lips, he said, "What did you do, walk? How'd you get here?"

"Somebody dropped me off."

"Who?"

"You don't know her."

"Her? Don't know her?"

"It was just somebody gave me a ride," Parker said. "What difference does it make?"

"I need a car," Nick said, low and fervent, as though

giving away a secret. Leaning forward, his whole body tense, he said, "I've got to get *away* from here. North, I can get into Canada, I can stop running for a while, figure out what to do next."

There was only one way Nick would stop running, but Parker didn't say so. Nodding at the gun, he said, "You've got that. That should help."

Nick looked at the gun with dislike. "I paid a lot for this, Parker," he said.

"I know that."

Nick made an angry shrug. "Some people," he said, "would rather be a hero than alive."

"That's not us."

"No." Nick stared at Parker, as though something about him were both mysterious and infuriating. Then, abruptly, he punched the gun butt onto the floor next to his leg, with a hollow *thud* that made him blink. "What are you *doing* here?" he demanded, as though it mattered.

"I wanted to look at the money."

"You wanted to *take* the money."

"Too soon for that," Parker said. If he kept showing Nick this bland face, reasonable, no arguments, maybe Nick would calm down a little, just enough to listen to sense. But probably not.

So, how to get to him from across the room? Five feet of wooden floor between them, with a gun at the far end.

Still calm, still with the same even voice, Parker said, "The law put it out that you got away from them before they could ask you anything. I didn't know if that was true or not. I figured, if the money's still here, it's true."

"It might have helped me with those people before," Nick said. "But not now."

"No, not now."

Nick shook his head, moving from anger to disgust. "You know how they got me."

"It was almost me," Parker told him. "If I hadn't heard about you, I would have been passing that stuff myself."

"I'd rather it was you," Nick told him, too caught up in his problems to pretend. "And I was the one that said, uh-oh, better throw that cash away."

"Just what I did."

"And came back *here*." Nick's confusion and exasperation and need were so intense he was forgetting the revolver, letting it point this way and that way as he gestured, trying to explain the situation to himself. "That's what I don't get," he said, staring hard at Parker. "That was over a *week* ago. You were out, you were free and clear, and you came *back*." Suddenly suspicious, he threw a quick wary look toward the door and said, "Is Nelson here?"

"No, Nick."

"Did *he* drive you? He's off getting some food, is that it?"

"I don't travel with McWhitney," Parker said. "You know that."

"I know you got a ride here," Nick said. "You got a ride here, and you're gonna stay a while, you're gonna sleep— Somebody's got to bring you food. Somebody with a car. Why don't *you* have a car?"

"I'm not gonna drive around this part of the world, Nick. I'm not gonna draw attention. I don't have good ID."

"You wouldn't even *be*—" Nick stopped and frowned, then said, as though suddenly seeing the answer to some riddle, "You're *waiting*."

"That's right," Parker said, and flipped the mat off his legs.

Nick clenched, the gun now pointing at Parker's eyes, trembling only a little. "Don't move!"

"I'm not moving, Nick. I got stiff, that's all, sleeping here."

"You could get stiffer."

"I know that, Nick." He's getting ready to shoot, Parker told himself. There's nothing more he's going to get from talking and he knows it. And he doesn't dare let me live.

"Parker . . ." Nick said, and trailed off, sounding almost regretful.

"We could help each other, Nick," Parker said. "Better for both of us. And I got water," he said, holding the bottle up in his left hand. "To keep me going till my ride gets here. It's just water. Check it out for yourself," he said, and slowly lobbed the bottle underhand, in an arc toward Nick's lap.

Nick looked at the bottle rising and falling through the air and Parker's right hand grabbed up a corner of the mat. He snapped the mat around at Nick's head, and his body lunged after it.

The bullet first went through the quilted mat.

TWO

1

One week earlier, just two days after the big armored-car robbery, Dr. Myron Madchen's week of horror began in earnest, and just when he'd thought his near-connection to the affair was buried and gone as though it had never been.

In a way, it *had* never been. He had not after all provided an alibi for one of the robbers, and he had not shared in the proceeds of the robbery. In fact, when the time finally came, he had had nothing to do with the matter. Everything had resolved itself with no action from him, and he was home free. Or so he'd thought.

That Sunday evening, two days after the robbery, he and Isabelle shared a fine dinner in a roadside restaurant called the Wayward Inn, where they cemented their plans for the future. A little patience was all they'd need. After all, the doctor was now a recent and unexpected widower, and it would be unseemly if he and Isabelle were publicly to make much of one another so soon.

So they'd driven to the Wayward Inn in separate cars, dined together, laughed together, gazed into each other's eyes, and parted with a chaste kiss in the parking lot. All the way home the doctor, a heavyset man in his fifties with thick iron-gray hair combed straight back and large eyeglasses, sang at the wheel, loud and off-key, a thing he'd never done before.

His house when he entered it seemed larger than before, and warmer. Also, it was empty, since he'd given Estrella a week off, with pay, feeling he'd rather be unobserved until he became more familiar with the new situation.

He'd forgotten to turn lights on when he'd gone out this evening. It hadn't been dark yet, and he wasn't used to the house being empty in his absence. Now he wanted light, all the light there was, and he went through the large house room by room, switching on lamps and track lighting and wall sconces and chandeliers everywhere, until he reached the small room off his bedroom, laughably known as his office—he'd be moving now to a larger space—and when he pushed the button for the ceiling light the voice in the corner said, "Turn that off."

He very nearly fainted. He clutched to the doorjamb so he wouldn't fall over, and stared at the robber.

One of the robbers, the one who'd been caught and then escaped, one of the two who'd threatened him last week when they were afraid he'd let something slip about their plans for the robbery. Which he was never going to do, never; it was important to him, too, or it had seemed vitally important before Ellen . . . had her heart attack.

"*Off.*"

"Oh! Yes!"

He'd been staring at the man, not even listening to what he'd said, but now he hit the button again and the room went back to semidarkness. The light from the bedroom behind him still showed his desk and chair, his filing cabinet, his framed degrees and awards, and in the darkest corner that hunched man in Dr. Madchen's black leather reading chair, just watching him.

"What—" He shook his head, and started again: "You can't be here."

"I can't be anywhere else," the man said. Dalesia; the television news had said his name was Dalesia.

"You can't be *here.*"

"Well, let's look at that, Doctor," Dalesia said. He was tense but in control, a hard and capable man. He said, "Why don't you go over and sit at your desk there, swivel the chair around to face me. Go ahead, do it."

So the doctor did it, and then, in a low and trembling voice, said, "I can't let anybody even know I know you."

"If I leave here, Doctor," Dalesia said, "I'm gonna be sore. I'm gonna be sore at *you*. And then, in a couple hours, a couple days, when the cops get me again, guess who I'm gonna talk about."

The doctor felt as though invisible straps were clamping every part of his body. He sat tilted forward, feet together and heels lifted, knees together, hands folded into his lap as though he were trying to hide a baseball. Slowly blinking at Dalesia, he said, "Talk about me? What could you say about me? I didn't do anything."

"You killed your wife."

The doctor's mouth popped open, but at first all he did was expel a little puff of air. But then, needing to have that accusation unsaid, never said, he protested, "That's— Nobody's even suggested such a thing."

"I will."

The doctor shook his head, still feeling those invisible bonds. "Why would anybody believe you?"

"They didn't do an autopsy, did they?"

"Of course not. No need."

"I'll give them the need." Dalesia was much more comfortable in this room than the doctor was. "If I stay here until the heat dies down," he said, "your wife had a heart attack. If I leave, you stuck her with a hypodermic needle."

"They *won't* believe you," the doctor insisted. "There's no reason to believe you."

"Doctor," Dalesia said, "we had our very first meeting about the robbery in your office. Your nurse and your receptionist saw me. You told us the money you'd get from us was your last chance, you were desperate, you had serious trouble." He shrugged. "Wife trouble, I guess."

"I was going to run away."

"Now you don't have to."

The doctor's mind filled with regrets, that he had ever involved himself with these people, but then regrets for the past were overwhelmed by horror of the present. What could he *do*? He couldn't force the man to leave, Dalesia really would take his revenge. Let him stay, and somehow find a way to stick *him* with a hypodermic needle? But Dalesia was tough and hard, he'd never give Dr. Madchen the opportunity. So what could he do?

Dalesia said, "There's a little bedroom downstairs, by the kitchen. Whose is that?"

"What? Oh, Estrella."

"Who's that, your daughter?"

"No, the maid, she's our maid."

"Where is she?"

"With her family in New Jersey. I gave her the week off."

"Well, that's good, then," Dalesia said. "I'll stay down there. I'll take off before this Estrella gets back, take your car, and that's the end of it."

"Oh, no," the doctor said. "You can't take my car!"

"I gotta have wheels."

"But you can't take my car."

"Why not? You report it stolen."

"But that would be the same thing," the doctor told him. "I'm safe because nobody's looking at me, that's what you said. I just had the one patient who was in the robbery with you, that's all. But if you tell them about me, they'll look at me." Dr. Madchen leaned earnestly forward. "Mr. Dalesia," he said, "this has all been an emotional nightmare for me. I'll let you stay, but when you go, steal someone else's car."

Dalesia nodded at him. "I could just kill you, you know."

Humbly, the doctor said, "I know you could."

Dalesia shook his head, as though angry with himself. "I'm not a nutcase," he said. "I'm not gonna hurt you unless I don't have any choice."

"I know that," the doctor said. "You can stay. Use Estrella's room. But please don't take my car."

"We'll see," Dalesia said.

The next week was harrowing, Dr. Madchen lived his normal life by day, doing his office hours in downtown Rutherford, seeing his patients, but always aware of that lurking demon waiting for him at home. If only he could just stay all night in the office, sleep on an examination table, eat at the luncheonette up at the corner.

But he didn't dare do anything outside his normal routine. Get up in the morning, eat breakfast with Estrella's closed door seeming to shimmer with what lay behind it, then go off to his office and return as late as possible at the end of the day.

He took Isabelle out to dinner twice that week, but the strain of this new secret was just too much for him. He couldn't possibly tell her what had happened. All he could do was wait for this horror to end.

At least the man Dalesia didn't intrude too much into the doctor's life. Estrella had her own television set and Dalesia seemed to spend most of his time in there watching it. From the sound, it was mostly the news channels. The doctor bought bread and cold cuts and cans of soup, and steadily they were consumed, but not in his presence.

The few times he did see Dalesia that week were unsettling, because it soon became clear that Dalesia was becoming more and more disturbed by the fix he was in. He'd gotten this far, to this temporary safety, but it couldn't last, and where could he go next? He had killed a US marshal, and every policeman in the Northeast was looking for him. The doctor began to fear that the man would eventually snap under the strain, that he would do something irrational that would destroy them both.

But it never quite happened, and on Friday evening, when Dr. Madchen got home and knocked on Estrella's door, Dalesia appeared in the doorway more haggard than tense, as though now the strain were robbing him of strength. "Estrella's coming back tomorrow," the doctor said. "I'm picking her up at the bus depot at three. You've been here almost a week. You really have to go."

"I know," Dalesia said, and half turned as though to look at the television set still running in the room behind him. "They're not letting up," he said.

"I've been stopped at roadblocks three times this week," the doctor told him.

Dalesia rubbed a weary hand over his face. "I gotta get away from here."

"Please don't take my car. It won't do you any good, and it can only—"

"I know, I know." Dalesia's anger was also tired. "I need a car, but I can't use one all the cops are looking for."

"That's right."

"Okay," Dalesia said. "Tomorrow, when you go get this Estrella, you're gonna drive me somewhere."

"Where?"

"I'll show you tomorrow," Dalesia said, and went back into Estrella's room, and closed the door.

2

Captain Robert Modale of the New York State Police was a calm man and a patient man, but he knew a whopping waste of time when it was dumped in his lap, and he'd been given a doozy this time. Irritation, which is what Captain Modale had to admit to himself he was feeling right now, had the effect of making him even quieter and more self-contained than ever. As a result, he had ridden in the passenger seat of the unmarked state pool car, next to Trooper Oskott at the wheel, all the way across half of New York State and probably a third of Massachusetts with barely a word out of his mouth.

Trooper Oskott, looking awkward and uncomfortable in civvies instead of his usual snappy gray fitted uniform, had tried to make conversation a few times, but the responses were so minimal that he soon gave up, and the interstates merely rolled silently by outside the vehicle's glass while Captain Modale contemplated this whopping waste of time he had to deal with.

Which was going to be a two-day waste of time, at that. The captain had to travel these hundreds of miles on a Friday, but he would reach Rutherford too late to meet with his Massachusetts counterparts until Saturday morning. In the meantime, the plan was that he and Trooper Oskott would bunk in a motel somewhere.

At first, though, it had looked as though no accommodation would be available, since it was the height of the fall foliage season over there in New England, and most inns of any kind were full. Captain Modale had been counting on that, the whopping waste of time called off for lack of housing, but then somebody made an early departure from a bed and breakfast with the disgusting name of Bosky Rounds, so the trip was on after all.

Bosky Rounds was not as repulsive as its name, though it was still not at all to the captain's taste. Nevertheless, the proprietor, Mrs. Bartlett, did maintain a neat and cozy atmosphere, steered the captain and the trooper to a fine New England seafood dinner on Friday night, and furnished such mountains of breakfast Saturday morning that the captain, indulging himself far beyond his normal pattern, decided not to mention the breakfast to his wife.

Mrs. Bartlett, in a side desk drawer in her neat office, seemed to keep an unlimited supply of local maps, on one of which she drew a narrow red pen line from where they were to the temporary unified police headquarters in the Rutherford Combined Bank building, that being the rightful owner of the money stolen last week.

When they went out to the car, they were preceded by another guest here, a brassy-looking blonde in black, who got into a black Honda Accord festooned with antennas. With just a quick glimpse of her profile, the captain found himself wondering, have I seen her before? Possibly in here last night, or at the restaurant. Or it could be she's just a kind of type of tough-looking blonde, striking enough to make you notice her, but also with a little warning sign in view.

Whatever the case, she was none of the captain's concern. He got into the pool car, and Trooper Oskott drove him over to the meeting.

What was normally a loan officer's space, a fairly roomy office with neutral gray carpet and furniture and walls, had been turned into the combined police headquarters, crammed with electronic equipment, extra tables and chairs, and easels mounted with photos, chain-of-command charts, progress reports, and particularly irritating examples of press coverage.

While Trooper Oskott waited at an easy parade rest out in the main banking area, still shut down since the robbery with all necessary bank transactions handled at another branch twenty-some miles away, Captain Modale went into the HQ room to be met by several of his opposite numbers, brought here at this hour specifically to meet with him.

What the captain read from those solemn faces and strong handshakes was a frustration even deeper than his own, and he decided to give up his bad temper at having his time wasted like this, because he knew these men and women were clutching at straws.

Three strangers had come into their territory, armed with antitank weapons illegal to be imported into the United States, and they'd made off with just about an entire bank's cash assets. One day later, the law had managed to lay its hands on one of the felons, but the very next day they lost him again, and lost one of their own as well. Now, in the nearly a week since, there had been no progress, no breaks, no further clues as to where any of the three men had gone.

One of the brass here to greet him, a Chief Inspector Davies, said, "I'll be honest with you, Captain, this reflects on every one of us."

"I don't see that, Inspector."

"Yes, it does," Davies insisted. "The one man we got, and I'm afraid lost—"

"*We* lost him," said the tight-lipped FBI agent Ramey that the captain had been introduced to. "We'll be changing some procedures after this."

"The point is," Davies said, "we know who he is. Nicholas Leonard Dalesia. He's not from the Northeast at all. He has no friends here, no associates, no allies. He hasn't stolen a car. He's been loose for almost a week in the middle of the biggest manhunt *we* can muster, and not a sign of him."

"He's gone to ground," said the captain.

"Agreed. But how? The feeling is, around here," the inspector told him, "the feeling is, the other two are with him."

"I don't follow that," the captain said.

"We know they had to leave the money behind, hide it somewhere," the inspector told him. "Are they with it now? One of them, the one you met, went over to New York State to engage almost immediately in another robbery. Did he do it for cash to tide the gang over while they're hiding out?"

"You're suggesting," the captain said, "the one that came to us managed to escape your manhunt, did that second robbery, and went right back *in*to the search area."

"You don't buy it," Inspector Davies said.

"I know *I* wouldn't do it," the captain said. "If I got my hands on some different money, I'd just grab it and keep going."

"Then where's Nicholas Leonard Dalesia? It just doesn't— Oh, Gwen, there you are. Come over here."

A very attractive young woman in tans and russets

had just entered the HQ room, and before the captain could show his bafflement—what was somebody like *that* doing here?—Inspector Davies all unknowing rescued him by saying, "Detective Second Grade Gwen Reversa, this is New York State Police Captain Robert Modale. You're the two law officers who've actually seen and talked to that second man."

After a handshake and greeting, Detective Reversa said, "John B. Allen, that's who he was when I met him."

"He called himself Ed Smith in my neighborhood."

She smiled. "He doesn't go in for colorful names, does he?"

"There's not much colorful about him at all."

"Tell me," Detective Reversa said, "what do you think of the drawing?"

"Of Mr. Smith?" The captain shook his head, "It works in the wrong direction," he said. "Once you know it's supposed to be him, you can see the similarities. But I had a conversation with the man *after* I saw those posters, and I didn't make the connection."

Inspector Davies said, "While you're here, Captain, I'd like you and Gwen to sit down with our artist and see if you can improve that picture."

"Because you think he's come back."

Detective Reversa said, "But you don't."

"I think," the captain said carefully, not wanting to hurt anybody's feelings, "the third man could very well still be here, helping Dalesia hide out. But the fellow I talked to? What do you think?"

"He's a cautious man," she said, "and not loud. No colorful names. I think he'd be like a cat and not go anywhere he wasn't sure of."

Inspector Davies said, "So the two of you could improve that drawing."

The captain bowed in acquiescence. "Whatever I can do to be of help."

The artist was a small irritable woman who worked in charcoal, smearing much of it on herself. "I think," Gwen Reversa told her, "the main thing wrong with the picture now is, it makes him look threatening."

"That's right," Captain Modale said.

The artist, who wasn't the one who'd done the original drawing, frowned at it. "Yes, it is threatening," she agreed. "What should it be instead?"

"Watchful," Gwen Reversa said.

"This man," the captain said, gesturing at the picture, "is aggressive, he's about to make some sort of move. The real man doesn't move first. He watches you, he waits to see what *you're* going to do."

"But then," Gwen Reversa said, "I suspect he's very fast."

"Absolutely."

The artist pursed her lips. "I'm not going to get all

that into the picture. Even a photograph wouldn't get all that in. Are the eyes all right?"

"Maybe," Gwen Reversa said, "not so defined."

"He's not staring," the captain said. "He's just looking."

The artist sighed. "Very well," she said, and opened her large sketch pad on the bank officer's desk in this small side office next to the main HQ room. "Let's begin."

The three had been working together for little more than an hour when Inspector Davies came to the doorway and said, "You two come listen to this. See what you think."

The larger outer room now contained, in addition to everything else, a quick eager young guy with windblown hair and large black-framed glasses like a raccoon's mask. He mostly gave the impression of somebody here to sell magazine subscriptions.

The inspector made introductions: "Captain Modale, Detective Reversa, this is Terry Mulcany, a book writer."

"Mostly fact crime," Mulcany said. He looked nervous but self-confident at the same time.

"That must keep you busy," the captain commented.

Mulcany flashed a very happy smile. "Yes, sir, it does."

The inspector said, "Mr. Mulcany believes he might have seen your man."

Surprised, dubious, the captain said, "Around here?"

"Yes, sir," Mulcany said. "If it was him."

The captain said, "Why do you think it was him?"

"I'm just not sure, sir." Mulcany shrugged in frustration. "I've been talking to so many people in this neighborhood this past week, unless I make notes or tape somebody it all runs together."

Gwen Reversa said, "But you think you saw one of the robbers."

"With a woman. Yesterday, the day before, I'm not really positive." Shaking his head, he said, "I didn't notice it at the time, that's the problem. But this morning, I was looking at those wanted posters again, just to remind myself, and I thought, wait a minute, I saw that guy, I talked to him. Standing . . . outdoors somewhere, with a woman, good-looking woman. Talking to them just for a minute, just to introduce myself, like I've been doing all week."

"And he looked like the poster," the inspector suggested.

"Not exactly," Mulcany said. "It could have been, or maybe not. But it was close enough, I thought I should report it."

Gwen said, "Mr. Mulcany, would you come over here?"

Curious, Mulcany and the others followed her into the side office, where the artist was still touching up the new drawing. Stepping to one side, Gwen gestured at the picture. The artist looked up, saw all the attention, and cleared out of the way.

Mulcany crossed to the desk, looked down at the drawing, and said, "Oh!"

Gwen said, "Oh?"

"That's him!" Delighted, Mulcany stared around at the others. "*That's* what he looks like!"

3

Nelson McWhitney liked his bar so much that, if the damn thing would only turn some kind of profit, he might just stay there all the time and retire from his activities in that other life. His customers in the bar were more settled, less sudden, than the people he worked with in that other sphere. His apartment behind the place was small but comfortable, and the neighborhood was working-class and safe, the kind of people who didn't have much of anything but just naturally watched one another's backs. About the only way anybody could get hurt really badly around here was by winning the lottery, which occasionally happened to some poor bastard, who was usually, a year later, either dead or in jail or rehab or exile. McWhitney did not play the lottery.

McWhitney did, however, sometimes play an even more dangerous game, and he was planning a round of it just now. When he got out of bed Saturday morning, he had two appointments ahead of him, both connected to that game. The second one, at eleven this morning, was a three-block walk from here to pick up the truck he'd bought yesterday, which would have the Holy Redeemer Choir name painted on the doors by then, and be ready for the drive north. And the first, at ten, was with a fellow he knew from that other world, named Oscar Sidd.

Because of the meeting with Oscar Sidd, McWhitney had only one beer with the eggs and fried potatoes he made in his little kitchen at the rear of the apartment before going out front to the bar, where he put a few small bills in the cash register to start the day.

He had the *Daily News* delivered, every morning pushed through the large letter slot in the bar's front door, so he sat at the bar and read a while, digesting his breakfast. He had some tricky moments coming, but he was calm about it.

Oscar Sidd was a frugal man; at exactly ten o'clock, wasting no time, he gave two hard raps to the glass of the front door, wasting no energy. A dark green shade was lowered over that glass, but this would be Oscar.

It was. A bony man a few inches over six feet, he wore narrow clothing that tended to be just a little too short for him. He came in now wearing a black topcoat that stopped above his knees with sleeves that stopped above the sleeves of his dark brown sport coat, which stopped above his bony wrists, and black pants that stopped far enough above his black shoes to show dark blue socks.

"Good morning, Nels," he said, and stepped to the side so McWhitney could shut the door.

"You okay, Oscar?"

"I'm fine, thank you."

"You want a beer?"

"I think not," Oscar said. "You go ahead, I'll join you with a seltzer."

"I'll join us both with a seltzer," McWhitney said, and gestured at the nearest booth. "Sit down, I'll get them." He wouldn't be introducing Oscar Sidd to his private quarters in back.

Oscar slid into the booth, facing the closed front door, opening his topcoat as McWhitney went behind the bar to fill two glasses with seltzer and ice and bring them around the end of the bar on a tray. He dealt the glasses, put the tray back on the bar, sat across from Oscar, and said, "How goes it?"

"Colder this morning," Oscar said. He didn't touch his glass, but watched McWhitney solemnly.

"You keep up with the news, Oscar," McWhitney suggested.

"If it's interesting."

"That big bank robbery up in Massachusetts last week."

"Armored car, you mean."

McWhitney grinned. "You're right, I do. You noticed that."

"It was interesting," Oscar said. "One of them got
picked up, I believe."

"And then lost again."

Oscar's smile, when he showed it, was thin. "Hard to
get reliable help," he said.

McWhitney said, "Did you notice how it was they got
onto him?"

"The bank's money is poisoned, I believe," Oscar
said. "Traceable. It can't be used."

"Well, not in this country," McWhitney agreed.

Oscar gave him a keen look. "I begin to see why
we're talking."

McWhitney, having nothing to say, sipped his
seltzer.

Oscar said, "You are suggesting you might have access to that poisoned cash."

"And I know," McWhitney said, "you do some deal-
ings with money overseas."

"Money for weapons," Oscar said, and shrugged.
"I am a...junior partner in a business trading
weaponry."

"What I'm interested in," McWhitney said, "is money
for money. If I could get that poisoned cash out of the
States, what percentage do you think I could sell it
for?"

"Oh, not much," Oscar said. "I'm not sure it would be worth it, all that trouble."

"Well, what percent do you think? Ten?"

"I doubt it." Oscar shrugged. "Most of the profit would go in tips," he said. "To import officials, shipping company employees, warehousemen. You start playing with those people, Nels, many many hands are out."

"It's an awful lot of money, Oscar," McWhitney said.

"It would very quickly shrink," Oscar said, and shrugged. "But since it's there," he went on, "and since you do have access to it, and since we are old friends"—which was not strictly speaking true—"it is possible we could work something out."

"I'm glad to hear it."

Oscar looked around at the dark wood bar. "Do you have this money with you now?"

"No, I'm on my way to get it."

"The police theory," Oscar said, "according to the television news, is that the thieves hid their loot somewhere near the site of the robbery."

"The police theory," McWhitney said, "is, you might say, on the money."

"But you believe," Oscar said, "you could now go to this area and retrieve the cash and bring it safely home."

"That's the idea," McWhitney said.

"And are you alone in this endeavor?"

"Well," McWhitney said, "that's the complication. There's other people involved."

"Other people," Oscar agreed, "do tend to be a complication. In fact, Nels, if I may offer you some advice . . ."

"Go ahead."

"Leave the money there," Oscar said. "The little profit you'd realize from an offshore trade becomes ridiculous if you have to share it with others."

"I may not have to share it," McWhitney said.

Oscar's thin face looked both amused and disapproving. "Oh, Nels," he said. "And do you suppose your partners have similar thoughts?"

McWhitney shook his head, frowning for a stressful instant at the scarred wood tabletop. "I don't think so," he said slowly. "Could be. I don't know."

"A dangerous arena to walk into."

"I know that much." McWhitney gave Oscar an impassioned look. "I'm not talking about *killing* anybody, Oscar. I'm not talking about a double-cross."

"No."

"You said it: a dangerous arena. If I have to defend myself I will."

"Of course."

"There's three of us."

"Yes."

"Maybe three of us come out with the money, maybe one of us comes out, maybe nobody comes out."

"You're determined to know which."

"Oh, I am," McWhitney said. "And so are the others. If at the end— If at the end, I'm clear of it, and I've got the money, and it's just me, I want to be able to think you'll be there for the export part."

"You won't be mentioning me to the others."

"No."

Oscar considered. "Well, it's possible," he said. "However, one caveat."

"Yeah?"

"If you come out trailed by ex-partners," Oscar told him, "I do not know you, and I have never known you."

"That's one thing I can tell you for sure," McWhitney promised. "I won't be trailed by any ex-partners."

4

Terry Mulcany couldn't believe his good luck. He'd been in the right place at the right time, that's all, and now look. Here he was in the exact center of the manhunt, hobnobbing with the major headhunters. Well, not exactly hobnobbing, but still.

Mulcany knew he didn't belong here. He wasn't at this level. A young freelancer from Concord, New Hampshire, he had two trade paperback true-crime books to his credit, both to very minor houses and both milking, to be honest, very minor crimes. A few magazine sales, a whole drawerful of rejections, and that was his career so far.

But not any more. This is where it all would change, and he could feel it in the air. He was an insider now, and he was going to stay inside.

If only he could remember where exactly he'd run into that robber and his moll. Outside some B and B around here, that's all he could bring to mind. A white-railed porch, greenery all around; hell, that described half the buildings in the county.

But even if he could never finally pinpoint where he and the robber had met, what he *did* remember was enough. He had come to this temporary police HQ just in time to end a disagreement between two of the top brass, and since it was the *top* top brass his evidence supported, he was in.

Apparently, it had been the local honcho, Chief Inspector William Davies, who believed one of the men they were looking for had left this area, pulled another robbery in New York State, and then come back here with the cash to finance the gang while they were hiding out. The other honcho, Captain Robert Modale from upstate New York, had insisted the robber, having safely gotten away from this area, would never dare come back into it. It was Mulcany's positive identification of the man that proved the chief inspector right.

Fortunately, Captain Modale didn't get sore about it, but just accepted the new reality. And accepted Terry Mulcany along with it. As did all of them.

The woman artist had left now, to have many copies made of the new wanted poster, and the others had moved into that office. Chief Inspector Davies sat at the desk where the artist had done her drawing, while Captain Modale and Detective Gwen Reversa—*there's* a picture for the book jacket!—pulled up chairs to face him, and Terry Mulcany, with no objection from the others, stood to one side, leaning back into the angle between the wall and the filing cabinet. The fly on the wall.

At first, the three law officers discussed the meaning of the robber's return, and the meaning of the woman who'd been seen with him, and the possibility the man was actually bold enough to be staying at one of the B and Bs nearby.

But what the sighting of the robber mostly did was put new emphasis on the whereabouts of the stolen money. "We probably should have done this before," Inspector Davies said, "but we're sure going to do it now. We'll mobilize every police force in the area, and we will search every empty house, every empty barn, every empty garage and shed and chicken coop in a one-hundred-mile radius. We will *find* that money."

"And with it, with any luck," Captain Modale said, "the thieves."

"God willing."

"Inspector," Mulcany said from his corner, "excuse me, not to second-guess, but why wasn't that kind of search done before now?" He asked the question with deference and apparent self-confidence, but inside he was quaking, afraid that by drawing attention to himself he was merely reminding them that he didn't really belong here, and they would rise up as one man (and woman) and cast him into outer darkness.

But that didn't happen. Treating it as a legitimate question from an acceptable questioner, the inspector said, "We were concentrating on the men. We were working on the assumption that, if we found the men, they'd lead us to the money. Now we realize the money will lead us to the men."

"Thank you, sir."

Detective Reversa said, "Captain, I don't understand what happened last weekend over in your territory. What was he doing there? Did he have confederates?"

Captain Modale took a long breath, a man severely tested but carrying on, "It really looks," he said, "as though the fella did the whole thing by the seat of his pants. If he ever had any previous connection with Tom Lindahl, we have not been able to find it. Of course, we can't find Tom Lindahl either, and unfortunately he's the only one who would know most of the answers we need."

Detective Reversa asked, "Tom Lindahl? Who's he?"

"A loner," Modale said, "just about a hermit, living by himself in a little town over there. For years he was a manager in charge of upkeep, buildings, all that, at a racetrack near there. He got fired for some reason, had some kind of grudge. When this fellow Ed Smith came along, I guess it was Tom's opportunity at last to get revenge. They robbed the track together."

Detective Reversa said, "But they're not still together. You don't think Lindahl came over here."

"To tell you the truth," Modale said, "I thought we'd pick up Lindahl within just two or three days. He has no criminal record, no history of this sort of thing, you'd expect him to make nothing but mistakes."

"Maybe," Detective Reversa said, "our robber gave him a few good tips for hiding out. Unless, of course, he killed Lindahl once the robbery was done."

"It doesn't look that way," Modale said. "They went in late last Sunday night, overpowered the guards, and made off with nearly two hundred thousand dollars in cash. None of it traceable, I'm sorry to say."

Inspector Davies said, "One hundred thousand dollars would be a good motive for the pro to kill this Lindahl."

"Except," Modale said, "his car was found Tuesday night in Lexington, Kentucky, two blocks from the bus depot there. People who travel by bus use more cash and fewer credit cards than most people, so he won't stand out. If he's traveling by bus and staying in cheap hotels in cities, spending only cash, he can pretty well stay out of sight."

Detective Reversa said, "How long can he go on like that?"

"I'd say," Modale told her, "he's already got where he wants to go. Anywhere from Texas to Oregon. Settle down, get a small job, rent a little place to stay, he can gradually build up a new identity, good enough to get along with. As long as he never commits another crime, never attracts the law's attention, I don't see why he can't live the rest of his life completely undisturbed."

"With one hundred thousand cash dollars," Inspector Davies said, sounding disgusted. "Not bad."

Oh, Terry Mulcany thought, if only *that* could be my story. Tom Lindahl and the perfect crime. But where is he? Where are the interviews? Where are the pictures of him in his new life? Where is the ultimate triumph of the law at the very end of the day?

No, Tom Lindahl was safe from Terry Mulcany as well. He would stay with the true crime he had, the armored car robbery, with bazookas and unusable cash and three professional desperados, one of them now an escaped cop killer. Not so bad, really.

THE LAND PIRATES; working title.

5

Oscar Sidd's car was so anonymous you forgot it while you were looking at it. A small and unremarkable four-door sedan, it was the color of the liquid in a jar of pitted black olives; dark but weak, bruised but undramatic.

Oscar sat in this car up the block from McW after his meeting with Nelson McWhitney. Some time today the man would set out on his journey to get the Massachusetts money. Oscar would trail him in this invisible car, and McWhitney would never know it. Out from beside the bar would come McWhitney's red pickup truck, and Oscar would slide in right behind.

Except it wasn't the pickup that emerged, it was McWhitney himself, from his bar's front door. He paused in the open doorway to call one last instruction to his bartender inside, then set off on foot, down the sidewalk away from Oscar Sidd.

That was all right. Oscar could still follow. He put the forgettable car in gear, waited till McWhitney was a full block ahead, then slowly eased forward.

McWhitney walked three blocks, hands in pockets, shoulders bunched, as though daring anyone or anything to try to slow him down. Then, taking his hands out of his pockets, he turned right and crossed the tarmac to a corner gas station that was also a body repair and detailing shop. He went into the office there, so Oscar stopped at the pumps and filled the tank, using a credit card. He expected to make a long drive today.

McWhitney was still in the office. When he came out, surely, he would be getting into one of the vehicles parked around the periphery here; but then which way would he travel?

The Belt Parkway was down that way, several blocks to the south; Oscar was going to guess that's where McWhitney would head, if his final goal was Massachusetts. Therefore, when Oscar left the station, he drove half a block north and made a U-turn into a no-parking spot beside a fire hydrant. He sat there and tuned his radio to a classical music station: Schumann.

Oscar Sidd was not as important in the international world of finance as he liked to suggest, but the reputation itself sometimes brought useful opportunities his way. This cash of McWhitney's now; that could be useful. In fact, he did have ways to launder hot money overseas, mostly in Russia, though the people you had to do business with were among the worst in the world. You were lucky to come away from them without losing everything you possessed, including your life. Still, McWhitney's money might be worth the risk. Oscar would trail along and see what opportunities might arise.

It was nearly ten minutes before McWhitney emerged, and then Oscar nearly missed him, it was so unexpected. A small battered old Ford Econoline van, a very dark green, with HOLY REDEEMER CHOIR in fairly rough white block letters on the door, came easing out of the gas station and paused before joining the moderate traffic flow.

It took Oscar a few seconds to realize the driver of the van, hunched forward to look both ways, was McWhitney, then the van bumped out to the roadway and turned right, just as Oscar had expected. He let one other car go by, to intervene between himself and the van, then followed.

The van up there was old, its bumper and the lower parts of its body pockmarked with rust, but the New York State license plate it sported was new, shiny, and undented. That name he'd seen on the door, Holy Redeemer Choir, that was also new, and must be the reason McWhitney had left the van at that shop.

Why would McWhitney use a name like that? What would it mean?

He wasn't surprised, several blocks later, when the van signaled for a right and took the on-ramp to the Belt Parkway, heading east and then north. We're going to New England, he thought, pleased, and the radio switched to Prokofiev.

6

The police meeting in the bank building was breaking up, and Gwen walked out to the main bank lobby with Captain Modale from New York State, saying, "I want you to know, Bob, I'm glad you made the trip over here."

"Somewhat to my surprise," the captain told her, with a little grin, "I am as well. All the way over here yesterday, I'll have to tell you the truth, I was in quite a sour mood."

They'd stopped in the lobby to continue their conversation as the others left. Gwen said, "You thought it was going to be a big waste of time."

"I did. Mostly, because I was convinced my Ed Smith was likely to be anywhere on earth except this neighborhood right here."

"I'm almost as surprised as you are," Gwen told him.

"When I talked with my John B. Allen, he just didn't seem like somebody who'd take unnecessary risks."

"I imagine," the captain said, "two million dollars could be quite a temptation."

"Enough for him to make a mistake."

"We can only hope."

"But now we've got a better likeness," Gwen said, "we maybe have more than hope. Which is the main reason *I'm* so glad you came over. We'll have the new poster up this afternoon, and if he's still in this general area we'll definitely scoop him in."

"I almost wish I could stay for it," the captain said. "But I'm sure you'll let us know."

"You'll be the *first* to know," Gwen promised him, and laughed. "I'll e-mail you his mug shot."

"Do." The captain stuck his hand out. "Nice to meet you, Gwen."

"And you, Bob," she said, as they shook hands. "Safe trip back."

"Thank you." The captain turned. "Trooper Oskott?"

The trooper had been seated at a loan officer's desk, reading a hunting magazine, but he now stood, pocketed the magazine, and said, "Yes, sir."

The two men left, and Gwen paused to get out her cell phone and call her current boyfriend, Barry Ridgely, a defense lawyer who spent his weekdays in court and his Saturdays on the golf course. When he answered now, in an outdoor setting from the sound of it, she said, "How many more holes?"

"I can do lunch in forty minutes, if that's what you want to know."

"It is. You pick the place."

"How about Steuber's?" he said, naming a country place that had originally been very Germanic but was now much more ordinary, the Wiener schnitzel and saurbraten long departed.

"Done. See you there."

Leaving the bank building, putting her cell phone away, Gwen turned toward her pool car when someone called, "Detective Reversa?"

She turned and it was Terry Mulcany, and it seemed to her he'd been waiting on the sidewalk specifically for her to come out. "Yes?"

"I've been waiting for you to come out," he said. "I have two questions, if you don't mind."

"Not at all. Go ahead."

"Well, the first is," he said, "I know my publisher, when the book comes out they're going to want pictures, and particularly the detectives who worked on the case. So what I was wondering is, if you've got a picture of yourself you especially like."

And have you, she wondered, asked the same question of the other detectives on the case? Of course not. Smiling, she said, "When the time comes, your editor can call me or someone else at my barracks. I'm sure there won't be any problem."

"That's fine," he said, with a hint of disappointment. What had he been hoping for? That she would suddenly hand him her *Playboy* playmate photo?

Wanting to get to Steuber's, she said, "Was there something else?"

"Yes. The other thing," he said, "is, I've been trying to remember where I saw that guy."

"My John B. Allen."

"Yeah." He twisted his face into a Kabuki mask, to demonstrate the effort he was putting in. "I don't know why," he said, "but there's something about a pear it reminds me of. The place where I saw them."

She did her own Kabuki mask. "A pear?"

"You know this area," he said, "a lot better than I do. Is there someplace around here called like the Pear Orchard, or Pear House, or something like that?"

"Not that I've ever heard of."

"Oh, well," he said, and elaborately shrugged. "If I figure it out, I'll give you a call."

"You do that," she said.

Barry's current client was a veterinarian who either had or had not strangled his wife. A jury would answer that question very soon now, probably early next week, and at lunch Barry was full of the problems besetting a poor defense counsel merely trying to put his client in the best possible light. "The judge just isn't gonna let me show the video in my summation," he complained, crumbling a roll in vexation. His client, in happier times, had won a humanitarian award from some veterinarian's association, and Barry insisted that no one who watched the video of the man's acceptance speech would ever he able to convict him of anything more nefarious than littering. "He's not even gonna let me show a *photo* of it."

"Well," Gwen said, being gentle, "that is kind of far from the subject at hand."

"Which of course is what the judge insists. But if I were to just *mention* it, the award, that could be even worse than—"

"Bartlett," Gwen said.

Barry frowned at her. "What?"

"Bartlett pear," Gwen said, "Mrs. Bartlett. Bosky Rounds."

"Gwen," he said, "is this supposed to be making sense?"

Beaming at him, Gwen said, "All at once, it does."

7

When Trooper Louise Rawburton signed in at the Deer Hill barracks at three fifty-two that afternoon, she was one of sixteen troopers, eleven male and five female, assigned to the four-to-midnight shift, two troopers per patrol car, doing this three-month segment with Trooper Danny Oleski, who did most of the driving, which was okay because it left her more freedom to talk. Danny didn't mind her yakking away, so it made for a happy patrol car, and if it wasn't for the system of rotation she knew she and Danny would have been happy as a team on their tours of duty forever.

However, the system of rotation was, everybody agreed, all in all a good idea. Put two straight men who get along with each other into the confines of a patrol car for several hours a day and they'll swap old stories, tell jokes, recommend movies and generally make the time go by. Make it one straight man and one straight woman and they'll do all the same things, but after a while they'll start to smile on each other a little differently, they'll start to touch, start to kiss, and down that road lies marital unhappiness and inefficient policing. A three-month rotation is usually short enough to keep that sort of thing from happening, to almost everybody's relief.

When Louise joined Danny and the other fourteen troopers in the shape-up room for the day's assignments from Sgt. Jackson, she expected today's tour to be more of the same: roadblocks. For over a week now, most of their on-duty time had been spent mounting roadblocks, the only variant being that the roadblocks were shifted to slightly different locations every day.

No one would say that the roadblocks had been completely unsuccessful. A number of expired licenses had been found, lack of insurance, faulty lights, the occasional drunk. But as to the *purpose* of the roadblocks, to nab the three men who'd destroyed three armored cars and made off with the fourth, full of cash, over a week ago, not a glimmer, The one man who'd been captured, and subsequently lost, was the result of a tip from a deli clerk who'd been passed one of the known stolen bills. Still, the powers that be felt better if they could mess up the whole world's schedules by littering the highways and byways with roadblocks, thus assuring the whole world that *something was being done*, so that's what Louise and Danny and the rest had been up to and would continue to do.

Except not. "This afternoon," Sgt. Jackson told them, pacing back and forth in front of where they stood on the black linoleum floor in the big square empty room with tables and chairs stacked along the rear, "our orders are a little different."

An anticipatory sigh of relief rose from the sixteen, and Sgt. Jackson gave a little shrug and said, "We'll see. Ladies and gentlemen, our mission has changed. We're not going to stand around any longer and wait for those fugitives to come to us. We are going to actively search for them by trying to find that stolen money."

One of the troopers said, "How we supposed to do that, Sarge? Hang out in delis?"

"Those three did not manage to transport their loot away from this part of the world," Jackson told him. "That's the belief we're operating from. Now, it's a big untidy pile, that money, and the idea is, if we look for it, we'll find it, and if we find it, the fugitives won't be too far away from it."

There was general agreement in the room on that point, and then Jackson said, "What our job is today, you are each getting a sector, and you are to physically eyeball every empty or abandoned building in that sector. Empty houses, barns, everything. On the table by the door there's a packet for each patrol, with your sector laid out in it, and by the way, a new suspect sketch on one of the fugitives. This is supposed to be closer to the real man."

"What'll they think of next?" asked a wit.

Riding shotgun, Louise ran an eye down the printout of the roads and intersections in their sector, then unfolded the new suspect sketch and studied it. "Oh, that one," she said.

Danny, driving, glanced once and away. "That one," he agreed.

"He doesn't look as mean this time," she decided.

"He was always a good boy," Danny said.

"Did somebody ever say that in a movie?" Louise wanted to know. "You hear it all the time."

"Beats me."

Putting away the sketch, Louise went back to the printout, studied it some more, and said, "We should start from Hurley."

"Real backwoods stuff."

"That's what they gave us. Oh!" she said, surprised and delighted, "St. Dympna!"

"Say what?"

"That's where I went to church, when I was a little girl. St. Dympna."

"Never heard of it," he said. "What kind of name is that?"

"She was supposed to be Irish. Most churches with

saints' names are Roman Catholic, but we weren't. We were United Reformed." Louise laughed and said, "The funny thing is, when they founded the church, they just wanted some unusual name to attract attention, so they picked St. Dympna, and then, too late, they found out she's actually the patron saint of insanity."

Danny looked at her. "You're putting me on."

"I am not. Turned out, there's a mental hospital named for her in Belgium. When I was a kid, that was the coolest thing, our church was named for the patron saint of crazy people."

"Is it still going?"

"The church? Oh, no, it got shut down, must be more than ten years ago."

"Ran out of crazy people," Danny suggested.

"Very funny. No, it's really way out in the sticks. There weren't so many small farms after a while, and people moved closer to town, until there was almost nobody left to go there, and nobody could afford to keep it up. It shut down when I was in high school. There was some hope an antiques shop would buy it, but it never happened."

"So that's got to be one of the places on our list."

"It sure is." Louise smiled in nostalgia, and looked at the road ahead. "I'm looking forward to seeing it again."

8

Mrs. Bartlett was sorry to see Captain Robert Modale and Trooper Oskott leave Bosky Rounds. Not that the room would go begging; this time of year, she always had a waiting list, and would surely fill that room again no later than Monday. But she'd liked the captain, found him quiet and restful, and a happy surprise after the unexpected departure of Mr. and Mrs. Willis.

The Willises had also been quiet and restful, not like some. Her in particular. Claire Willis. Mrs. Bartlett never did get a good reading on her husband, some sort of humorless businessman who clearly didn't really care about anything but his business and was taking this vacation solely to make his wife happy; which was of course a mark in his favor.

But the rest was all her. She did all the driving and all the talking, and even made the apologies when they unexpectedly had to depart because of some crisis back home with his business.

Mrs. Willis had been so apologetic and so understanding, even offering to pay the unused portion of their stay, that Mrs. Bartlett couldn't even get irritated. Of course she refused the extra payment, and assured Mrs. Willis she'd fill the room in no time, and then, the Willises barely gone and before she'd even had time to turn to her waiting list, here came the call from the New York State Police, needing a room for just the one night.

It was a sign, Mrs. Bartlett felt. She and Mrs. Willis had behaved decently toward each other, and this was Mrs. Bartlett's reward. She certainly hoped Mrs. Willis was rewarded, perhaps with something other than that cold-fish husband of hers.

Barely half an hour after the departure of Captain Modale, here came Gwen Reversa, looking as fresh and stylish as ever, though Mrs. Bartlett could never quite get over her feeling that an attractive young woman like Gwen was never supposed to be a policeman. Still, here she was, carrying yet another of those wanted posters. Mrs. Bartlett frankly didn't like the look of those things, and felt they did nothing for the decor and atmosphere of Bosky Rounds, but there was apparently to be no choice in the matter. Her front room was a public space, and the public spaces must willy-nilly be filled up with these dreadful-looking gangsters.

Still, she couldn't help saying, "*Another* one, Gwen? I'm not going to have much wall left."

"No, it's a replacement," Gwen told her, going over to where the two drawings and one photograph were already tacked to the wall. "You know that Captain Modale who was here."

"A charming man."

"Well, he and I both encountered the same one of the suspects. This one," she said, taking the latest poster from its manila folder and holding it up for Mrs. Bartlett to see. "We worked together with the artist," she said, "and we think this picture is much closer to the real man. See it?"

Mrs. Bartlett didn't want to see it. Squinting, nodding, she said, "Yes, I see it. It takes the place of one of the others, does it?"

"Yes, this one. Here, I'll take the old one with me." While she was tacking the new poster in the old one's place, she said, "Did a reporter named Terry Mulcany talk to you?"

"Oh, the true-crime person." she said. "Yes, he was all right. He seemed awfully rushed, though."

Gwen turned away from the wall, folding the old poster and putting it into her coat pocket as she said, "He thought he possibly saw that man somewhere around this house."

"In *this* house? Gwen!"

"Not in the house, near it. Outside. With a woman."

"Gwen," Mrs. Bartlett said, and pointed toward the row of posters, "not one of those people has ever set foot in Bosky Rounds. Can you imagine? What on earth would they ever do *here*?"

"Well, they have to sleep somewhere."

Frosty, Mrs. Bartlett said, "*Those* are not my customers, Gwen."

Laughing, Gwen said, "No, I suppose not. Still, if you see anybody who looks like that," and pointed again at the new poster, "be sure to call me."

"Of course. Of course I will."

Gwen left, and Mrs. Bartlett spent the next few minutes sending out e-mails to her waiting list, telling them an unexpected five-day vacancy had just come up. As she was finishing that, Ms. Loscalzo, from number two upstairs at the back, came through, heading out, carrying her usual big ungraceful black leather shoulder bag. "Off for more scenery," she said, as though it were a joke, or a difficult chore of some kind.

"Enjoy the day, dear," Mrs. Bartlett said.

"That's a good idea," Ms. Loscalzo said, waved, and marched off.

Mrs. Bartlett couldn't help but wonder about Sandra Loscalzo. Most tourists this time of year were couples or groups, almost never singles. You'd go to the movies or a museum by yourself, but you wouldn't drive around the countryside looking at the changing leaves all on your own in your car. Anyway, most people wouldn't.

Also, Ms. Loscalzo seemed a little coarser, a little more—Mrs. Bartlett was almost ashamed of herself, thinking such a thing—working-class than most of the leaf peepers she'd seen over the years. And she didn't wear a wedding ring, though that didn't necessarily mean anything. It could be she was recovering from having been recently divorced, and needed a change to get her just for a little while out of her regular life. That might be it.

As she thought about Sandra Loscalzo, Mrs. Bartlett found herself unwillingly gazing at the posters of the wanted robbers, diagonally across the room from her desk, and especially that new one, nearest her along the wall.

Oh, my goodness. She stared at the poster, then rose and walked over to frown at it from a foot away.

It couldn't be. Could it? Could that nice Claire Willis be married to *that*? It was impossible.

But it was true. The more she stared at that cold face, the more she saw him standing there, just behind his wife, saying little, showing almost no emotion, certainly no enthusiasm for looking at leaves.

But why would Claire Willis be married to a bank robber? It was ridiculous. Mrs. Bartlett would be more willing to believe Sandra Loscalzo was married to such a man; not Claire Willis.

There had to be an explanation. Maybe the police had their eye on the wrong man all along, or maybe this was just as inaccurate a sketch as the first one. They got it wrong before, maybe they got it wrong again.

Should she phone Gwen, let the police detective sort it out? Mrs. Bartlett had the uneasy feeling that was exactly what she should do now, but she didn't want to. It wasn't Henry Willis she was thinking of, it was Claire. She didn't want Gwen glaring down her nose at Claire Willis. Whatever was in the woman's life, Mrs. Bartlett certainly didn't want to be the one who made things worse. She couldn't call Gwen because she couldn't make trouble for that nice Claire Willis.

And there was a second reason as well, even stronger than that, though she barely acknowledged it to herself. But the fact is, she had been very remiss. Oh, yes, she'd assured Gwen, over and over, she had studied those posters, she was ready to do her civic duty if any of those robbers happened to wander into Bosky Rounds.

But had she studied? Had she paid attention? The man had been right *here*, in this house, in this room, and she had never noticed. How could she possibly make that phone call now and say, "Oh, Gwen, I just happened to notice . . ."

No. She couldn't do it. She couldn't phone Gwen, not now, not ever, and the reason was, she was just too embarrassed.

9

Sandra drove south and east out of town, headed for the Mass Pike. When McWhitney had phoned her this morning from Long Island he'd told her their new truck was an Econoline van, dark green, not black, and he expected to get to her around five. She hadn't told him she'd bird-dog him the last part of the trip, but that's what she intended to do. Always err on the side of caution, that was her belief.

She'd expected two or three roadblock stops along the way, but yesterday's heavy police presence had suddenly evaporated. Where had they gone? Had they caught Nick again? If so, she and McWhitney were going to have to rethink their approach to the money in the church, and Parker might already be in trouble over there. She turned on the car radio, looking for all-news stations, but heard about no developments in the search for the robbers.

So where were all the cops? Sandra didn't like questions without answers. She had half a mind to just keep driving south, and let this whole business alone.

Well, she could still bird-dog McWhitney. If something seemed weird with him, or if he got nabbed by the cops, she'd be long gone.

There were two gas stations near the turnpike exit he'd be taking. She chose the one in the direction he would go, parked among a few other cars along the side perimeter, and used her hands-free cell to call him in the truck.

"Yeah?"

Of course he wouldn't say hello like everybody else. Sandra said, "Just wondering how you're coming along."

"Fine."

That was helpful. "About how long, do you figure?"

"You're impatient for that green, huh?"

"I don't wanna be doing my hair when you get here."

That made him laugh, and loosen up a little. "Do your hair tomorrow. I'll be there in less than an hour."

"Where are you now?"

"On the Pike, be getting off in five, ten minutes."

"I'll be here," she promised, and broke the connection, and spent the next seven minutes watching traffic come down the ramp and peel away.

If Roy Keenan were still alive, and still her partner, he'd be waiting north of here right now for Sandra to tell him when the van came off the turnpike and what it looked like. Then he'd follow from in front, keeping the van visible in his rearview mirror, so that Sandra could hang well back, ignoring the van as she watched for other interested parties. But Roy was gone and hadn't as yet been replaced, so she'd do it this way.

Sandra had gotten her private investigator's license a year after leaving college, and had worked for the first few years mostly on unimportant white-collar criminal matters for a large agency with many business clients. She investigated inside-job thefts at department stores, trade-secret-selling employees, minor frauds, and slippery accounting.

The work, which had at first been interesting, soon became a bore, but she couldn't find an acceptable alternative until, at a fingerprinting refresher course given by the FBI, she'd met Roy, whose previous woman partner had just left him to get married. "Well, that won't happen to me," Sandra assured him.

They became a very good partnership. She kept her private life to herself, and Roy was fine with that. Sometimes they were flush and other times money was tight, but they'd never been scraping the bottom of the barrel until this protracted, expensive, frustrating search for Michael Maurice Harbin, a search that *still* hadn't paid off, and the reason she was now waiting for an extremely dangerous felon in a Ford Econoline van.

There. Very good, good choice, a dark green beat-up little van. Holy Redeemer Choir.

She started the Honda, gave the van a chance to roll farther down the road to the north, then started to ease out after him, but abruptly stopped.

She'd almost missed him, dammit, she must be more distracted than she'd thought. Because there he was, in a little nondescript no-color car, just easing into McWhitney's wake.

What he'd done, this guy, he'd come down the ramp and stopped at the yield sign at the bottom, even though there wasn't any traffic to yield to. He stayed there almost ten seconds, a long time, until a car did come along the secondary road going in his direction. Then he pulled in behind that car. Sandra knew that maneuver, she'd done it herself a hundred times.

Now she accelerated across the gas station tarmac to the road, so she could get a close-up of the tail as he drove by. Cadaverous guy in black, hunched forward, very intense, very focused.

Sandra did the same thing he'd done, waited for another car to intervene, then joined the cavalcade. Out here there were towns to go through, every one of them with one traffic light. The first time they were all stopped at a light she took a hurried look at her Massachusetts map, then when they started moving again she called McWhitney and said, "You've got a tin can on you, you know about that?"

"What? Where are you?"

"Listen to me, Nelson. He's in a nothing little car, two behind you."

"Jesus Christ!"

"Tall bony guy in black, looks like he's never had a good meal in his life."

"That son of a bitch."

"You know him, I take it. Pal of yours?"

"Not any more."

"Okay."

"Don't worry, Sandra, I'll get rid of him."

"Not in that truck," Sandra told him. "We don't want any problems with that truck. I'll deal with it."

"The dirty bastard."

"Up ahead, you got Route 518."

"Yeah?"

"Take the left on 518, the right on 26A, right on 47, it'll take you back to this road, then just head on up, same as before."

"And you'll be up there."

"I'll do the cutout, catch up with you later. Here comes 518."

The traffic light up ahead was green. The van's turn signal went on, and then the follower. They went off to the left, and Sandra continued north, saying to McWhitney, "You wanna tell me about him?"

"His name is Oscar Sidd, he's supposed to know about moving money out of the country."

"You told him what we've got."

"So we'd have some place to take it after."

"And you just happened to forget to mention your friend Oscar to me."

"Come on, Sandra. I never thought he'd pull something like *this*. What does he want, something to fall off the back of the truck?"

"If he forgot to mention to you, Nelson, that he was gonna take a drive up here today, he wants more than a skim, doesn't he?"

"The bastard. He's out of his league, if that's what he's thinking."

"He is and it is. If you see me, a little later, don't slow down."

"There you go insulting me again."

"Have a nice ride, Nelson," she said, and broke the connection.

A few minutes later she was stopped at the red light for the intersection with Route 47. When it turned green, she drove more slowly, looking for a place to roost, and found it at a small wooden town hall on the edge of town, up a rise higher than the road. Saturday afternoon, it was deserted, no cars in the parking lot beside the building. She pulled in there, up the steep driveway to the parking lot beside the town hall, then swung around to face south, opened the passenger window, and waited.

Not quite ten minutes, and here came the van. Well behind it, but with no intervening vehicle this time, came Oscar Sidd in his no-brand jalopy. Sandra popped the glove compartment and took out her licensed Taurus Tracker revolver, chambered for the .17HMR, a punchier cartridge than the .22, in a very accurate handgun.

As the van went by, Sandra leaned over to the right window, curled her left hand onto the bottom of the frame, the side of her right hand holding the Tracker on the back of her left, and popped a bullet into Oscar Sidd's right front tire.

Very good. The car jerked hard to the right, ran off the shoulder, and slammed into the rise, jolting to a stop. The windshield suddenly starred on the left side, so Mr. Sidd's head must have met it.

Sandra started the Honda, closed the right window, put the Tracker away, and drove back down to the road. When she went past the other car, its hood was crumpled and steaming, and Mr. Sidd was motionless against the steering wheel.

Redial. "Nelson?"

"What's happening?"

"That's me behind you now. See me?"

"Oh, yeah, the black waterbug."

"Thank you. Can you find that church from here?" Because she wasn't sure she'd be able to.

"Sure."

"Then I'll stay back here," she said, "keep an eye out, see are there any more friends of yours coming along."

She did recognize the road the church was on, when McWhitney turned into it, and hung back even farther than before. There had still been no roadblocks, though she had seen the occasional police car, moving as though with a purpose, not just idly on patrol.

What had changed in the world? She'd considered talking it over with McWhitney and decided it was better not. If everything was okay at the church, fine. If it turned out there was some sort of trouble there, let McWhitney walk into it, at which point Sandra would just drive on by, nothing to do with that van, and head for Long Island.

There it was, church on the right, white house on the left. McWhitney turned in at the house, because that's where Parker would be, and Sandra lagged back so far that McWhitney was already out of the van, looking impatient, before she pulled in beside him. She opened her door, McWhitney said, "You wanna take a lotta time here?" and a gunshot sounded from the house.

10

It had been the worst week in Nick Dalesia's life, but it never quite went entirely all to hell. Every time things looked hopeless there'd be one more little ray of possibility, just enough to get him moving again. He was beginning to think that hopelessness was the better option. More restful, anyway.

Public transportation had seemed like the best way to get clear of the search area right after the robbery. Who knew that all he had to do to get himself scooped up like a marlin in a net was buy a sandwich to eat on the bus to St. Louis, paying for it with a twenty from the bank?

He was certain he was done for then, with all those lawmen's hands on his elbows, and he spent the first night in the solitary holding cell at some state police building in western Massachusetts trying to figure out what he could trade for a better deal.

The money certainly. McWhitney: he could point a finger right directly at that bar of his. And Parker, he could give them leads on him, too. And the story of the killing of Harbin for wearing the federal wire, and the names of the other people present at that meeting. There was a lot he could give them, when he added it all up. He was still going to do serious time, and he knew it, but he'd be a little more cushioned than if he'd walked in empty-handed.

But then, early next morning, they didn't question him at all, so he didn't get to tell them which top lawyer they should call, who happened to be a guy Nick didn't know but had read about in the newspapers, and who would be perfect for Nick's defense, and who would be bound to take the job because this was a high-profile case and that was a lawyer who liked high-profile cases.

But then none of that happened, and then, early in the morning, he was rousted out and put into a small office with a cup of coffee and a donut. It was the US marshals who had their hands on him, and they didn't care to question him about anything, they were just there to conduct him to someplace else.

One marshal in the room, an automatic sidearm in a holstered belt strapped over his coat, his partner gone off to see about transportation. The coffee was too hot to drink, so Nick threw it in the marshal's face, grabbed the automatic, whammed the guy across the forehead with it, and headed for the door.

Locked. The marshal must have a key. Nick turned back and the guy was conscious, coming up to a sprawled seated position, groping in a dazed way inside his coat, coming out with something.

The son of a bitch had another gun! Nick lunged across the space between them, shoved the automatic barrel into the guy's chest to muffle the sound, and shot him once.

All the guy had needed to do was lie there till Nick was out of the room, then yell like an opera singer, but no. Nick found the keys, and got moving.

Getting through and out of that state police building had been very tough. It was a maze, and the alarm was already out. He eventually went out a window to a fire escape and down to where he could jump onto the roof of a garage, and then get to the ground and gone.

He kept the automatic. He'd paid for it, he'd paid a lot, and he was gonna keep it.

He carjacked an early-morning commuter drinking his cardboard container of coffee at a red light, but he couldn't keep that vehicle long; just enough time to get to some other town. And while he drove, he tried to think where to go next.

Forget transportation, public or otherwise. Any traveling he did would get him picked up right away. What he had to do was go to ground and stay there, maybe a week, maybe even longer.

But where? Who did he know in this part of the world? Where would he find a safe place to hunker down?

He was just about to abandon his carjacked wheels when he remembered Dr. Madchen. Not a criminal, not somebody the police would have any reason to look at. But Nick did have a handle on his back, because the doctor had some kind of connection with the local guy in the setup of the robbery, and the doctor would provide him an alibi.

When, just before the robbery, it had looked as though the doctor was calling attention to himself, being coy, being stupid, Nick and Parker had gone to his home to have a word with him. That was all it took, and in any case the robbery went wrong so quickly there was no alibi in the world that would help the local guy and so, after all, the doctor did nothing. Which meant he was clean; but if Nick asked him to help, he would help.

The week at the doctor's house was grueling. Nick had a terrific sense of urgency, a need to take action, but there was never anything to do. All week the television news told him the heat was still on, and he knew he was the reason why. If it was just the bank's money, they'd ease off after a while, but he'd killed one of their own, and they weren't about to let up.

He kept trying to make plans, come to decisions,

but there was simply not a single move he could make. If he left Dr. Madchen's house, how long would it take them to catch up with him? No time at all. But how could he stay here, like this, as though his feet were nailed to the floor?

He had never thought before that he might some day go crazy, but now he did. The jangling electric need to *do* something, *do* something, when there was nothing to be done; there was nothing worse.

He thought sometimes he'd kill the doctor, take his car and whatever valuables he had in the house, and head north. But then he'd remember the roadblocks, and he knew it couldn't happen. He didn't have safe ID. They had his *picture*. What was he going to do?

By Friday evening, when the doctor told him the maid would be coming back tomorrow and Nick couldn't stay at the house any longer, Nick was ready to go, it hardly mattered where. He'd been more beaten down by the week of inaction than if he'd spent a month in a war zone. When the doctor gave him the ultimatum—too timid for an ultimatum, but that's still what it was—he actually welcomed it, as a change, any change from being in this paralysis, and he knew immediately what he was going to do.

"Tomorrow," he told the doctor, "when you go get this Estrella, you're gonna drive me somewhere," and the next day he had the doctor drive him past the church, but without stopping or pointing it out or making it seem as though the church had anything to do with his plans. But then, a little farther on, where the road curved and dipped down to a bridge over a narrow stream, Nick said, "Stop here, I'll get out and you drive on."

The doctor stopped, beside the road just before the bridge, and Nick got out, then stooped to look back into the car and say, "We never met each other, Doctor. If you make no trouble for me, I'll make no trouble for you."

"I won't make any trouble."

Nick believed him; the doctor's face looked as whipped as his own. "Thanks," he said, and shut the car door, and the doctor's Alero wobbled away over the bridge and out of sight.

Nick saw no other cars as he walked back to the church. Would it all be the same? He was counting on it. His idea, if it could even be called an idea, was to grab as much of the money as he could, steal a car from somewhere around here, then drive it strictly on back roads, keeping away from the roadblocks.

Canada was still the best hope he had, if he had any hope at all. He'd head north, up through the winding little roads in the mountains. He'd sleep in the car and only use the bad money in places where he would immediately be moving on, paying only for food and gas.

Somewhere up near the border he'd have to leave

that car and walk, however far it was until he reached some town on the Canadian side. There, he could do a burglary or two to get some safe Canadian money, steal another car, and make his way to Toronto or Ottawa. There he could come to at least a temporary stop, and try to figure out the rest of his life from there. It wasn't much of a plan, but what else did he have?

The church looked the same. When they'd first holed up in here, McWhitney had kicked open the locked side door so they could carry the boxes of money in, then they'd kicked it shut again so that it looked all right unless you really examined it. Had anything been done to change that? Not that Nick could see. He leaned on the door and it fell open in front of him.

The money was still there, up in the choir loft, untouched. Nick filled his pockets, then went downstairs and outside, this time not bothering to pull the door shut.

He was going to keep walking down the road, looking for a vehicle parked outside somebody's house or a passing driver to carjack, when he glanced at the house across the road and decided it wouldn't hurt to see what might be inside there that could be of use. He expected the place to be empty, but was quiet as a matter of habit, and when he walked into one of the upstairs bedrooms somebody was asleep in there, on the floor, covered with a rough-looking quilt.

A bum? Nick edged closer, and was astonished to see it was Parker.

What was Parker doing here? He had come for the money, no other reason.

So where was his car? Nick had been on both sides of the road and he hadn't seen any car. Was it hidden somewhere? Where?

He hunkered against the wall, across the room from Parker, trying to decide what to do, whether he should go look for the car, or wake Parker up to ask him where it was, or just kill him and keep moving, when Parker came awake. Nick saw that Parker from the first instant was not surprised, not worried, not even to wake up and find somebody in the room with a gun in his hand.

We used to be partners, Nick thought, with a kind of dull disbelief. Could we be partners again? Could we get out of this mess together?

We're not partners, he thought, as Parker looked at him with that lack of surprise and said, "So there you are." I don't have partners any more, Nick thought. I only have enemies now.

"Where's your car?" he asked.

Parker bullshitted him. He danced around without moving, without trying to get up from the floor, just saying things, dancing around. He doesn't have a car. But why doesn't he have a car? Somebody dropped him off, some woman dropped him off, some woman Nick doesn't know dropped him off.

Bullshit! Where did this woman come from, all of a sudden? Why is Parker asleep *here*? Now angry, angry at Parker, at the marshal, at the world, Nick pounded the pistol butt on the floor and demanded, "What are you *doing* here?"

"I wanted to look at the money."

"You wanted to *take* the money."

No, Parker told him, no, too early for that. And more bullshit, more bullshit, while Nick tried to figure out what Parker was up to.

"You were out, you were free and clear, and you came *back*." With sudden tense suspicion, with a quick shiver up the middle of his back, he said, "Is Nelson here?"

But Parker said no, he didn't travel with McWhitney, and Nick could believe that. But what was he *doing* here? With sudden conviction, Nick said, "You're waiting."

"That's right," Parker said, and as though it didn't matter he flipped that rough quilt off his legs.

Nick didn't like that movement. He didn't like any movement right now. Aiming the automatic at Parker's face, on the brink of using it, only holding back because he needed to know what was going on here, who was Parker waiting for, where was there a *car* in this for Nick, he aimed the automatic at Parker's face and yelled, "Don't move!"

"I'm not moving, Nick. I got stiff, that's all, sleeping here."

"You could get stiffer," Nick said, and as he said it he knew he couldn't wait any more. He didn't care about Parker any more, didn't need the answers to any questions, didn't have any questions left.

But Parker was still talking, moving his hands now, saying they could help each other, saying, "And I got water," holding up a clear bottle in his left hand.

Water? What did Nick care about water? But he looked at the bottle.

"It's just water. Check it out for yourself," Parker offered, and slowly lobbed the bottle toward him underhand, in a high arc, toward the ceiling, toward his lap.

Nick's eyes followed the movement of the bottle for just a second, for one second too long, and something like a great dark wing slashed across the room at him, Parker lost and hidden behind it, the quilt twisting toward him through the air. He fired, with nothing to aim at, and a hard hand chopped down on the gun wrist. The automatic skittered away across the wood floor and Parker's other hand clawed for his throat. Nick screamed, kicked his heels to the floor to jolt himself away, flopped over to his right, found his elbows and knees beneath himself, and lunged out and away, up off the floor and through the closed window.

THREE

1

Parker reached for that fleeing body, but the hours spent asleep on the floor had left him too stiff, his movements less coordinated than he was used to. He missed Nick entirely, and watched him crash through the window, the force of his impact taking out the wooden crosspieces and mullions, shattering the glass, leaving a jagged hole with fresh wind blowing in.

Cursing the stiffness, Parker turned the other way and grabbed the automatic off the floor. Then he used the wall to help him to his feet, and hobbled to the gaping window.

Nick was out of sight. He'd landed on weedy lawn back here, twelve feet down, with the woods half a dozen fast paces away.

Fresh blood hadn't yet darkened on the zigzag edges of glass. Nick was hurt out there. How badly?

A sound on the stairs, behind him. Had Nick come *in*? Without his gun?

Parker moved to the corner farthest from the doorway and waited. He heard the heavy steps coming up the stairs, and then silence. He waited.

"Parker?"

Parker leaned against the wall behind him. "Nelson," he said.

McWhitney appeared in the doorway, his own gun loosely in his hand, but reacted when he saw what Parker was carrying: "Whoa! What's this?"

"Nick's gun," Parker pointed at the slashed window. "That was Nick."

"He was *here*?"

"In and out."

"We heard the crash. Sandra went around back." Crossing to the wrecked window, he said, "How come he didn't do you?"

"He wanted to know where my car was."

McWhitney laughed, first surprised and then amused. "The greedy bastard. Where's he been keeping himself the last week?"

"He didn't say."

McWhitney leaned forward to look out the window and down, and call, "What do you see?"

"Broken glass," Sandra called back. "Broken wood. What happened up there?"

"Nick went out the window."

"Nick?"

"We'll come down," McWhitney told her.

They went downstairs and around to the back, to find Sandra standing where Nick must have landed, frowning away to the woods behind and to the right of the house. Turning to them, she said, "What happened here?"

"I was asleep," Parker said, "and then Nick came in. He wanted a car."

"You don't have a car," Sandra told him.

Parker shrugged. "We discussed it. Then I got his gun, and he went out the window."

"You didn't push him out."

"I didn't want him out. I wanted him in there."

McWhitney said, "We gotta find him now, Parker."

"I know."

"Wait a second," Sandra said. "We're here, we've got the van. Let's pick up the money and get *out* of here."

"Sandra," McWhitney said, "Nick has run out his string. Wherever he was holed up, he isn't there any more. He's on foot, he's cut up from that window, he's a dead duck. If the cops get their hands on him, he puts me right out of business. The bar, everything. I'm on the run the rest of my life." To Parker he said, "You, too."

"Not so much."

"Enough. Enough to give your friend Claire some nervous moments."

"That's true."

Sandra said, "What are you gonna do, run around in the woods? You're not gonna find him in there. Maybe he's bleeding to death."

"We can't take the chance," McWhitney said.

Sandra thought about it, and realized she had to bend on this. "Five minutes."

Parker said, "Sandra, we'll give it what it takes."

"I'll be with the cars," she told them. She was disgusted.

"With your piece in your lap," McWhitney advised.

"Now you're insulting *me*."

She headed off around the house and Parker walked over to where dry fallen leaves had been recently scuffed, showing streaks of wetter leaves beneath. The streaks pointed at an angle away from the right rear corner of the house.

Parker and McWhitney, both with guns in their hands, followed the streak line's direction, away from the house. They kept parallel to each other, but a few paces apart. Away from the house, the narrow tall scrubby second-growth trees were like an army of lancers, all upright, with daylight in vertical strips between. The ground was rocky and uneven, but trended upward, with clusters of thorny shrubs intermixed with nearly bare areas of grass and weed.

They walked along the scrub ground for two or three

minutes, watching in every direction, and then McWhitney stopped and said, "I'm not seeing anything."

"Neither am I."

Parker looked back and the house was almost completely hidden back there, just a few hints of white. "We don't have him," he said.

Complaining, McWhitney said, "I'm not a tracker, I'm a bartender. This isn't where I do my best work."

They turned around, headed back to the house, and Parker said, "When you get home, just in case, you gotta start building an alibi."

"Oh, I know. What's that?"

Ahead and to their left, a piece of dark gray cloth flapped, its corner stuck to the thorny lower branch of a wide-spread multiflora rose. They went over to look at it, and Parker said, "That's the pants he was wearing."

"The road's right over there."

"I know it. There's blood on these thorns here."

"The son of a bitch is hurt," McWhitney said, "but he won't stop. Can we get to the road this way?"

"If we want to bleed like Nick. Easier back around by the house."

They retraced their steps to the house, and when they came around the side of it Sandra got out of her Honda and said, "Give me some good news for once."

"We're alive," McWhitney told her.

"Try again."

Parker looked at the van with HOLY REDEEMER CHOIR on the doors. "Looks good."

Sandra said, "So why don't we use it?"

Parker told her, "You drive your car and the van over to the church, we'll take one look along the road for Nick."

She heaved a sigh, to show how patient she was. "Done," she said.

They walked along the road while she shuttled the vehicles behind them. A red pickup went by, with two guys in hunting caps in it, neither of them Nick; everybody waved.

In a ditch there was a space of tangled smears where somebody or something had slid down out of the roadside scrub, maybe fallen here, then moved on. Impossible to say which direction he had taken.

McWhitney said, "I could take Sandra's car, follow down this road. Or she could, while we move the boxes."

"Waste of time," Parker said. "You can't find a man on foot with a car. We just get the cash, and clear out of here."

As they walked back toward the church McWhitney, sounding irritated but resigned, said. "Alibi. Parker, I'm gonna have to call in every marker I got out. And just hope it turns out enough people owe me something."

2

Sandra had everything ready. The van, its rear doors open, was backed against the concrete landing and steps that led to the side door McWhitney had kicked in more than a week ago. She'd moved her Honda farther forward along that side wall of the church, facing out, tucked in close enough to the church to block from the road much of the view of what would be going on between doorway and van.

McWhitney approved: "Good work."

"You boys do the heavy lifting," she said. "I'll sit in my car and watch. If I see something I don't like, I'll honk twice. And then probably drive like hell."

Parker said, "If they're that close, you shouldn't run away. You should draw on us and make a citizen's arrest."

"That's right, Sandra," McWhitney said. "You're the upright citizen. You've got licenses and everything."

"Just what I always wanted," she said. "Caught in the cross fire. Start: let's get out of here."

They started. They had a lot of weight to carry, boxes of money and boxes of hymnals, out of the choir loft, down the stairs and into the van. To their right, Sandra sat in her Honda with the engine on, the radio playing soft rock as she read a *Forbes* magazine.

The money boxes and hymnal boxes were different brands of the same kind of mover's carton, white, rectangular, with deep-sided lids fitting over them, like the boxes seen carrying evidence into federal courtrooms. Since the hymnals had been on top upstairs, for camouflage, most of them had to be moved first and set aside so the money boxes could be loaded into the van. They developed a two-man bucket brigade system, so they wouldn't get in each other's way on the stairs, and within half an hour the van was two-thirds full, with more money boxes still upstairs.

"We'll have to leave those," Parker said. "We need space for the other boxes in front and on top, to show at the roadblocks."

"I hate to leave any of it," McWhitney said, "but you're right."

There were four money boxes still upstairs. They restacked hymnal boxes on top of them, then went down to finish loading the van and, as they did, Parker saw a streak of mud on the floor that hadn't been there before. It was near the closed door to the basement, a place they'd holed up in after the robbery, a one-time community room from which all the appliances had been removed.

They each carried a carton of hymnals out to the van and Parker said, "You keep working, I got something to do."

McWhitney was curious, but kept working, as Parker moved forward to Sandra in the Honda and said, "I need a flashlight."

"Sure," she said, and took one from a small metal box of supplies she kept bolted to the floor in front of the seat, to the right of the accelerator. "What for?"

"Tell you when I get back."

The basement, as he remembered it, would be pitch-black, because it had plywood panels that slid across in front of the windows, for when they used to show movies down there. That meant he wouldn't be able to open the door at the head of those stairs without Nick, down below, knowing he was coming down.

Why would Nick come back *here*, of all the places in the world? Maybe he still thought there was some chance he could find an edge for himself. Or maybe he just didn't have any place else to go any more. Maybe his life was a maze, and this was the far end of it, and he didn't have any other choices.

Parker opened the door, slid through, shut the door behind himself. As dark as he remembered. He silently went down two steps, then sat on that step and waited.

Nick wouldn't have another gun, but he might have something.

No light down there, no sound. Parker waited, then abruptly there was a sound, and an instant later light; gray daylight. Nick was sliding back one of the plywood panels, baring a window. Maybe he thought that would level the playing field somehow.

Parker put the unnecessary flashlight on the step behind him, stood, and took the marshal's automatic from his pocket.

Nick said, "Hold it, Parker. You want to see this. Take a look out there. I mean it, take a look."

"At what?"

Nick backed away from the window, gesturing for Parker to help himself. "Do yourself a favor," he said.

Parker went down the rest of the stairs, crossed to the head-high window, and looked out at a state police patrol car, stopped in front of Sandra's Honda, just blocking it. Two uniforms were getting out of the patrol car, shrugging their gunbelts at their waists as they moved toward Sandra, one of them a man, the other a woman, both white.

Looking at the automatic in Parker's hand, Nick said, "You don't want to make any loud noises. Not now."

3

Had Sandra honked twice, when she saw the patrol car, as she'd said she would? If so, Parker hadn't heard it down here. Concrete-block walls, room mostly underground, plywood over the windows. But a shot would be something else. Cops would hear a gunshot.

"We don't want them looking in that window," he said, and slid the plywood closed with his right hand as his left hand reached for Nick.

"Hey!"

Nick had backpedaled, but his shout told Parker which way he was moving. And then his ragged breath gave him the spot, and then Parker had his hands on him.

This had to be fast, and then he had to find that window and slide the plywood open just far enough so he could find his way back to the stairs and collect the flashlight. Bring it back, shut out the daylight again, switch on the flash, shine it quickly around.

There. Across the rear end of the room had been a kitchen. The appliances were long removed, making broad blank insets in the Formica counter that ran all across the back, but the sink was still there, set into the counter, with closed cabinet doors beneath. They opened outward to the left and right, with no vertical post between them.

Parker opened the cabinet doors and saw that the pipes for the sink were under there, but nothing else. Plenty of room.

He dragged Nick across the linoleum floor, bent him into the space under the sink, and shut the doors. Then he went back upstairs and outside, where the male cop was giving McWhitney back his license and registration and the female cop was looking at one of the hymnals from a carton in the van.

"Hello," Parker said, and they all looked at him. He nodded at Sandra and said. "There's nothing down there."

"Good," she said, and explained to the cops, "This is Desmond. He's the other volunteer."

"I'm in recovery," Parker said.

The male cop said, "You were in the basement?" Nobody interrogates somebody in recovery.

"We wanted to know if there was anything useful down there," Parker said. "But it's been cleaned out."

To Sandra he said, "The refrigerator's gone, dish-washer, everything."

The female cop pointed at the flashlight Parker carried. "No electricity in there?"

"No water, nothing." He looked over his shoulder at the building. "Empty forever."

"Not forever," she said, and surprisingly smiled. "I went to this church when I was a little girl."

Sandra, delighted by the news, said, "You did? What was it like?"

They all had to discuss that for a while. Parker saw that Sandra had toned herself down, made herself look softer, and that both cops had bought into the idea that she was connected to some sort of religious mission on Long Island, and that he and McWhitney were rehabilitated roughneck volunteers.

After the reminiscence about the old days at the church wound down, the male cop said, "Louise, do we have to toss this place? These people have been all through it."

"Maybe I'll just peek in," Louise said. "See what it looks like now."

"It looks sad," Sandra told her. "Been empty a long time."

Louise frowned, then shook her head at her partner. "Maybe I don't wanna go in."

"I think you're right," he said, and told the others, "We'll let you people finish up here."

Louise said, "I'm glad the hymn books are going to a good home anyway."

Sandra said, "Would you want one? You know, as a reminder."

Louise was delighted. "Really?"

"Sure, why not?" Sandra grinned at her. "One hymn book more or less, you know?"

Louise hesitated, but then the male cop said, "Go ahead, Louise, take it. You can sing to me while I drive."

Louise laughed, and Sandra handed her a hymnal, saying, "It couldn't go to a better person."

McWhitney said, "Could I ask you two a favor?"

"Sure," said the male cop. His partner hugged the hymnal to her breast.

"We're driving a little truck," McWhitney pointed out. "Just what everybody's looking for. If we're gonna get stopped by all these roadblocks, we're not gonna get back to Long Island until Tuesday. If you could get the word—"

"Oh, don't worry about that," Louise told him. "The roadblocks are stopped."

"They are?"

"That's why we're out here," Louise said. "We're searching every empty building in this entire area."

"Not for the fugitives," the male cop said. "For the money."

"It has to still be somewhere around here," Louise

explained. "So this is a change of policy. The idea is, if we find the money, we'll find the men."

"That makes sense," Sandra said. "Good luck with it."

"Thanks."

The cops moved off, Louise holding her hymnal. They got into their patrol car, waved, and drove off. McWhitney watched them go, then said, "Good thing they didn't start that new policy yesterday." Looking at Parker he said, "We can throw those prayerbooks out of the van now. We get to take the rest of the money after all."

4

No, you don't," Sandra said.

McWhitney glowered at her. "How come?"

"You're still two guys in a truck," she told him. "They don't have to have roadblocks to see you drive by and wonder what you've got in there."

"Sandra's right," Parker said. "And we've got to move. Those two are going into the house across the way."

They watched as, across the road, the two cops left the patrol car, went up on the porch, tried the door, and stepped inside.

Sandra said, "What do they find in there?"

Parker said, "A broken window, and your mat."

"I can live without the mat."

McWhitney said, "What if Parker drives your car? Then we're a man and a woman in a truck."

"I'll drive my car," Sandra told him.

Parker said, "I'll ride with Sandra. We'll follow you,

and we've got to go *now*. They're gonna find blood on the broken window. New blood."

McWhitney was fast when he had to be. He nodded, slammed the van doors, and headed for the cab of the truck. Parker and Sandra passed him on their way to the Honda, and Parker said, "Head east."

"Right."

Sandra got behind the wheel, Parker in on the other side. She started the engine, but then waited for McWhitney to drive around her and turn right, toward the bridge over the little stream. As she followed, Parker looked back at the white house. The two cops were still inside.

"They'll call in reinforcements," he said. "But they won't come from this direction."

"I wondered why you wanted to go east."

Up ahead, McWhitney jounced over the bridge, the van wallowing from all the weight it carried. The Honda took the bridge more easily, and Sandra said, "Did Nelson tell you about the guy who followed him?"

"Guy? No."

"Oscar Sidd."

"Never heard of him."

"Nelson says he's somebody knows about moving money overseas. Nelson talked to him about our money, but he didn't expect Oscar to follow him."

"Oscar thought he'd cut himself in."

"That was the idea."

"And Nels's idea, talking to him in the first place was, cut us out."

"I noticed that, too."

"What happened to Oscar?"

"I popped a tire, left him in a ditch."

"Alive?"

"I don't kill people, Parker," she said. "All I shot was his tire. He maybe got a concussion from the windshield, but that's all."

"So he's out of the picture. Fine."

Sandra said, "How long do we go east?"

"You can talk to Nels, can't you?"

"On our cells, sure."

"Tell him, we'll be coming to a bigger road soon. He should turn right and look for a diner or someplace where we can stop and talk."

It was a bar, a sprawling old wooden place with mostly pickup trucks out front, a pretty good Saturday afternoon crowd at the bar, and an active bumper pool table in the open area to the bar's left. On the other side were some booths. Pointing to them, McWhitney said, "Grab a place. I'll buy."

Parker and Sandra picked a booth, and she said, "You want to drive the whole way tonight?"

"Away from here, anyway. Let's see what Nels thinks."

"The thing is," Sandra said, "my stuff is still in my room at Mrs. Chipmunk's. But if I go there, that leaves you being two men in a truck again."

McWhitney came back, his big hands enclosing three beer glasses. Putting them on the table, he bent low and said, "Drink up and we'll get outa here." Then he sat, next to Parker.

Parker said, "Something?"

"You see behind the bar," McWhitney said, "those posters. It's you and me and Nick again."

"They've been around all week."

"They got a new one of you over there," McWhitney said. "I hate to tell you this, but it's a lot closer."

Sandra said, "How'd they do that? It better not be Mrs. Chipmunk. I don't want to walk into a lot of questions about who do I associate with."

"You'll talk your way out of that," Parker told her. "But we've got to decide." To McWhitney he said, "Sandra has to go back to the place where she's staying, her stuff is there."

"So you and me travel together, you mean." McWhitney shook his head. "Back to matching the profile."

"If that new picture's that good," Parker said, "I can't chance a traffic stop. Sandra, you've got to drive me some more. Once we're south of the Mass Pike, we're out of the search area, we'll be okay. Drive me down there, then come back up. I'll go on with Nels, and you'll catch up with us at his place later."

"Another two hours in the car," she said. "That's just great."

5

They were still north of the Mass Pike, in hilly forested country with darkness beginning to spread, when a northbound state police car did a kind of stutter as it passed them, and Parker said, "He's coming back."

Sandra looked in her mirror. "Yep. His Christmas tree went on. I guess I should do the talking."

"No," Parker said. "He doesn't want us, he wants the van. Don't volunteer. If we stop, he'll throw a light on me."

Sandra eased to the shoulder to let the cop go by, saying, "I don't like to leave McWhitney alone."

"With the money, you mean. But that's okay. He won't run out on us, he's too tied to that bar of his."

"Then what was he gonna do with Oscar?"

Up ahead, McWhitney pulled off the road, the cop sliding in behind him. Parker said, "He was gonna kill us with Oscar, if he could. Or else just let it play out and see what happens. If it falls that way, he can suddenly say, 'Oh, here's a guy can help.'"

"You have nice friends," Sandra said.

"He's not my friend."

Sandra drove over the hilltop and down the other side, and far ahead of them, downslope, the Mass Pike made a pale band of footlights between the darkening ground and the still-bright southern sky.

"I'm gonna stop there," Sandra said, and nodded ahead toward an old grange hall converted to an antiques shop. An OPEN flag in red, white, and blue hung from a short pole slanting upward above the entrance. Two cars were parked in the small gravel lot at the side. She drove in, parked closer to the road than to the other cars, and watched the rearview mirror. After five minutes she said, "It shouldn't take this long."

"Maybe Nels doesn't look right for the part."

"I'm going back."

She U-turned out of the lot and drove back over the hill.

There had been two troopers in the patrol car, both now out. One stood beside McWhitney's open window, holding his license and registration, talking to him. The other had the rear doors of the van open. Two of the hymnal boxes were on the ground behind the van, their tops at a tilt. The trooper was leaning forward into the van, moving boxes, trying to see if there was anything else inside there. McWhitney's face, when they drove by, was bunched like a fist with his effort to stay calm and impassive.

"They didn't like his looks," Parker said.

"All that trooper has to do," Sandra said, "is see there's two kinds of boxes in there."

Parker looked ahead along the road, but in this direction there were no antiques shops, no buildings at all, just the bright-leaved trees on both sides, reflecting the last of the daylight. "Just pull off on the shoulder," he said, "If it looks like they're calling for backup, we're getting out of here."

"You know it."

She angled them onto the shoulder and stopped, lights off and engine running, then watched the scene behind them in her mirror, while Parker adjusted the outside mirror on his side so he could also see what was going on.

There wasn't a lot of traffic at the moment on this two-lane road, and the few cars that did pass in either direction just went on by the stopped van and patrol car with its flashing lights. They were used to seeing troopers stop other drivers.

Finally the troopers decided to give up. The one handed McWhitney his papers, while the other stood and waited at the rear of the van, hands on his hips. Then the two walked back to their patrol car, with the lights still flashing on its roof. They left the two boxes of hymnals on the ground behind the open rear doors of the van.

"They're not neat," Sandra said.

"They're punishing him for making them not like him," Parker said, "and then for not giving them a reason to pull him in."

The troopers got into their car, its flashing lights went off, and they steered out past the van and away. Once they were out of sight, McWhitney, furious, came thumping out of the van to put the boxes back.

Parker said, "Drive over there."

Sandra made the U-turn, and they pulled in to a stop behind the van. Just as McWhitney finished stowing the boxes and shutting the doors, Parker opened his window and called, "We'll stop at a motel down by the Pike. This is enough for today."

"More than enough," McWhitney said, and stomped away to get behind the wheel.

Sandra didn't wait for him. She pulled out onto the road and ran them south again, saying, "I'll drop you at the motel, but then I'm done."

"I know."

"I'll stay in touch with McWhitney, find out what's happening with the money."

"You can tell your friend to come back from her vacation now."

Sandra laughed. "I already did."

6

It was a chain motel with an attached restaurant and bar. Before dinner, Parker and McWhitney met for a drink in the bar, where Parker gave him cash to cover his room, since McWhitney had put the whole thing on his credit card. "It's getting harder to operate without plastic," McWhitney commented.

"I'm getting new when we're done with this."

The bar was mostly empty, a dim low-ceilinged place with square black tables and heavy chairs on dark carpet. A young waitress in a short black skirt brought them their drinks, and McWhitney signed the bill. When she left, Parker said, "I think I may know somebody who could take care of the money."

"Somebody to take it off our hands?"

"He probably could," Parker said. "But he might not want to. We had a disagreement the last time around. But he's a businessman, he might go along with it."

"Who and what is he?"

"A guy named Frank Meany. He works for a liquor import outfit in Jersey called Cosmopolitan Beverages. They're mobbed up and they do a lot of under-the-counter stuff. Some of it is with Russia."

"That sounds good. How come you didn't say anything about him before?"

"We didn't have the money before. Until I've got something to trade, I've got nothing to say."

McWhitney nodded. "What was the disagreement?"

"They involved themselves in somebody else's argument, somebody thought he had a beef with me." Parker shrugged. "I convinced them to get uninvolved."

McWhitney laughed. "Stuck their nose in somebody else's business, and you gave it a little bop."

"Something like that. I'll try calling him tomorrow. If he tells me to go to hell, fine, I can't blame him. If he says, sounds good, let's meet, it could either mean it sounds good and he wants a meet, or he's holding a grudge and wants another crack at me."

"But you figure this is a better bet than Oscar Sidd."

"Maybe. Worth a try anyway."

"And I bet you want me along, if the guy says okay, no hard feelings, let's meet."

"That's right." Parker gestured over his shoulder. "Without the money."

7

Around eleven Monday morning, Parker took Claire's car, still the rental Toyota, to the gas station not far from her house where he usually made his phone calls, to avoid leaving records on Claire's line. It was a process that required nothing more than patience and a lot of change. It was an exterior pay phone on a stick at the edge of the gas station property, unlikely to be observed or tapped. In this rural setting, there was little to draw anybody's attention.

"Cosmopolitan Beverages, how may I direct your call?"

"Frank Meany."

"Who shall I say is calling?"

"Parker."

There was a little pause. "Is that all?"

"He'll know," Parker said.

The operator was gone a long time, and when she came back she said, "Mr. Meany's in confer—"

"Tell him we both know all about that."

"Sir?"

"Tell him we talk now, or we don't talk. I won't call back."

"Sir, I can't—"

"Tell him."

It was a shorter wait this time, and then the remembered voice of Frank Meany came on the line, a hard, fast, tough-guy voice. "I thought we were done with one another."

"You mean the little trouble. That's all over. Everything's fine now."

"But here you are on the phone."

"With a business deal."

There was a little shocked silence, and then: "A *what*?"

"I need expertise and a particular kind of access," Parker said, "and I think you're the guy has it."

"Which expertise would that be?"

"Frank, do you really like long conversations on the phone?"

"I don't like long conversations with *you*."

"Up to you."

Parker waited while Meany tried to work it out. Meany was a hard-nosed businessman in that gray area where the legal part of what he did, importing hard and soft drinks from various parts of the world, spread a protective blanket over the illegal part. He wasn't his own boss, but worked for a man named Joseph Albert whom Parker had talked to on the phone that last time but had never met face-to-face. The conversation with Albert had been about how much of Albert's business he was willing to lose before backing away from his confrontation with Parker. The first asset Parker had been offering to remove was Meany. Happily for everybody, Albert had seen there was no reason to be a romantic; cut your losses, and go.

Would Meany still resent that? Of course. Would he be ruled by his resentment? Parker was betting he was too realistic for that.

Finally Meany said, "You wanna come *here* again? I'm not sure I want you here." *Here* being the corporate offices and warehouse of Cosmopolitan, in a bleak industrial area of the Jersey flats just south of where the New Jersey Turnpike Extension, a steel and concrete slab miles long, rose high and blunt over the industrial scree to the Holland Tunnel.

Parker said, "No, I don't need to go there. Up in the northern part of the state, you know, off the Garden State Parkway, there's a state park. They got a picnic area there, right in front of the park police building. When people have lunch there, they feel very safe."

"I bet they do," Meany said. He sounded sour.

"I bet you and me, just you and me, I bet we could both get there today by two o'clock."

"From here? Sure. What's in it for me?"

"That's what we're gonna talk about."

Meany considered that, and then said, "A little picnic lunch with you, in front of the park police."

"But out of earshot."

"Yeah, I got that. All right, No First Name. I'll see you at two o'clock."

"Brown-bag it," Parker said.

His second call was to McWhitney's cell phone. "He's on. Two o'clock."

"I'll be in red."

8

Parker was the first to arrive. Leaving his car in the parking area, carrying a deli-bought Reuben-on-rye sandwich and a bottle of water in a brown paper bag, he chose a picnic bench midway between the facade of the low brick park police building and the narrow access road around to the parking area. He sat with the building to his right, access road to his left, parking area ahead.

It was a bright day, but a little too cool for lunch in the open air, and most of the dozen other picnic tables were empty. Parker put the paper bag on the rough wood table, leaned forward on his elbows, and waited.

The red Dodge Ram pickup was next, nosing in and around the access road to park so the driver was in profile to the picnic area. Then he opened a *Daily News* and sat in the cab, reading the sports pages at the back.

Parker would have preferred him to move to a table, as being less conspicuous, but it wasn't a problem.

The next arrival might be. A Daimler town car, black, it had a driver wearing a chauffeur's cap, and it stopped on the access road itself. The driver got out to open the rear door, and Frank Meany stepped out, looking everywhere at once. He was not carrying a brown bag.

Meany said a word to the driver, then came on, as the driver got back behind the wheel and put the Daimler just beyond the red pickup. A tall and bulky man with a round head of close-cropped hair, Meany was a thug with a good tailor, dressed today in pearl-gray top-coat over charcoal-gray slacks, dark blue jacket, pale blue shirt and pale blue tie. Still, the real man shone through the wardrobe, with his thick-jawed small-eyed face, and the two heavy rings on each hand, meant not for show but for attack.

Meany approached Parker with a steady heavy tread, stopped on the other side of the picnic table, but did not sit down. "So here we are," he said.

"Sit." Parker suggested.

Meany did so, saying, "You're not gonna object to the driver?"

"He gets out of the car," Parker said, "I'll do something."

"Deal. Same thing for your friend in the pickup."

"Same thing. You didn't bring a sandwich."

"I ate lunch."

Parker shook his head, irritated. As he took his sandwich out of the bag and ripped the bag in half to make two paper plates, he said, "People who ride around in cars like that one there forget how to take care of themselves. If I'm looking at you out of one of those windows over there, and you're not here for lunch, what are you here for?"

"An innocent conversation," Meany said, and shrugged.

"In New Jersey?" Parker pushed a half sandwich on a half bag to Meany, then took a bite of the remaining half.

Meany lifted a corner of bread, "Reuben," he decided. "Good choice." Lifting his half of the sandwich, he said, "While I eat, you talk."

"A couple weeks ago, up in Massachusetts, there was an armored car robbery. The news said two point two million."

"I remember that," Meany said. "It made a splash."

Parker liked it that Meany didn't want to rehash their last meeting, because neither did he. He said, "They caught one of the guys right away, because it turned out they had all the money's serial numbers."

"Tough," Meany said. His small eyes watched Parker as intently as if Parker were a tennis match.

"The people who have the money can't spend it," Parker said.

Meany put what was left of his sandwich down onto the paper bag. "You're saying you have it."

"No, I'm saying you have business overseas."

Meany thought about that, and slowly nodded. "So the way you're thinking about it, I could take this money and make it meld into the international flow and just be anonymous again."

"That's right."

Meany thought about that, looking off toward the Palisades. "It might be possible," he said.

"Good."

"And then we'd share whatever I got out of it."

"No," Parker said, "it wouldn't work like that. You'd buy it from us and we'd go away."

Watchful, Meany said, "What price are you thinking about?"

"Ten cents on the dollar. In front."

"And the take on this robbery was over two mil?"

"There was some slippage. Call it two even."

"Two hundred grand." Meany said, and shook his head. "I couldn't give you all that in front."

"I can't get it any other way."

Meany said, "Yeah, but what are you gonna do if I just say no?"

Parker said, "You fly to Europe sometimes. You go business class, right?"

"So?"

"Anybody else in the plane?"

Laughing, Meany said, "I get it. There's gotta be other customers out there. Where's this money now?"

"Long Island."

"So you got it out of Massachusetts."

"That's right."

"And now you're ready to trade. This was north of two mil? How can I be sure?"

"Read the news reports. Look, Meany, I'm saying ten percent on the dollar. You can't get a steeper discount than that. If the final number's a little off, one way or the other, who's gonna complain?"

Meany thought about it. "And you're gonna want cash."

"Real, unmarked, and unstolen."

Meany laughed, "That's what we usually deal in. I'm gonna have to consult."

"With Mr. Albert."

Meany didn't like the reminder. "That's right, you had that phone call with Mr. Albert. He didn't like it I let you get that close to him."

"No choice."

Meany nodded, "Well, Mr. Albert's a sensible man," he said, "He understood I didn't have any other choice either."

"Good. So he might like this."

"He might, I might not mention the vendor's you."

"That's all right with me."

"I thought it would be," Meany said. "So where do I get in touch with you?"

Parker looked at him. "I like the way you never give up," he said. "When should I call you?"

Meany grinned. He was liking the conversation more than he'd thought he would. He said, "You got any time problems on your hands?"

"No. Where it is it's safe for as long as we want."

"Too bad. I'd rather you were under the gun."

"I know that."

Meany thought it over. "Call me Thursday," he decided. "Three in the afternoon."

"Good."

Meany waved a hand over the sandwich remnants. "We don't have to do lunch," he said.

Massachusetts

Two and a half weeks after the big armored car robbery, and still neither the robbers nor the money had been found. No one would admit it, but law enforcement was no longer completely committed to the hunt. The track was cold, and so was the case.

On that Monday afternoon, troopers Louise Rawburton and Danny Oleski were nearing the end of an eight-a.m.-to-four-p.m. tour, when they passed St. Dympna United Reformed Church. Louise happened to be driving at that moment, Danny every once in a while insisting she take a turn, so she braked when she saw the church and said, "There it is again."

Danny looked at it. "So?"

"I wanna see it," she said, and pulled off the road to stop beside the church. "I'm sorry we didn't go in there last time."

"Well, we were kind of busy last time. And we had to report that broken window across the road."

"Well, we're not busy now. Come on, Danny."

So Danny shrugged and they both got out of their cruiser, adjusted their belts, and went up to the broken side door. It was early twilight here at this time of year, still plenty of light, but it would be dark inside the church, so they both carried their flashlights. They pulled the door open and stepped in, their light beams shining across the rows of pews and, near the doorway, three of the hymnal boxes squatted on the floor.

"Looks like," Danny said, "they couldn't fit them all."

"Suppose we should take these? Donate them to somebody."

"We can take them back to the barracks anyway," Danny said.

"Good idea."

Aiming the flashlight this way and that, he said, "It's a real shame. This building's still in good shape."

Louise bent to one of the boxes and tugged. "These things are heavy," she said.

"Well, yeah, they would be. Books."

"Maybe we should just take some of them now," she said. "Be sure there's anybody wants them."

"Just take one book," Danny said. "They're not going anywhere."

Louise lifted the top off the box she'd been trying to lift, and they both looked in at the rows of greenbacks. The two flashlight beams trembled slightly, converging on all that money.

"Oh, my God," Danny whispered.

"Oh, Danny," Louise wailed, "Oh, no, Danny, it was *them.*"

"We talked with them," Danny said. He was wide-eyed with shock. "We stood out there and we talked with them."

"That goddamn woman gave me a *hymnbook.*"

Danny's flashlight suddenly spun around, to fix on the basement door. "Why was he down *there*?" he asked. "What was he doing down *there*?"

Bitterly, Louise imitated the guy who'd come up out of the basement. "Oh, there's nothing down there. Appliances all gone, everything gone."

"Louise," Danny said, "what was he *doing* down there?"

She had no answer. He walked over to that door and pulled it open and shone the flashlight down the stairs. Then he uselessly clicked the light switch a few times. Then his nose wrinkled and he said, "Jesus Christ. What's that smell?"

Detective Gwen Reversa knew there were times she received an assignment only because she was a woman, and was thought therefore to be of a more sympathetic nature than the average male cop. She didn't disagree with the assessment, but it irritated her anyway. She would have preferred gender-blind assignments, but when the woman's touch was wanted, she knew she was always going to be that woman.

In her current case, for instance, she was clearly the only one in the office even considered to take the squeal. It was a wrongful death emerging out of a long-term case of simple slavery. The perps were a middle-aged Chinese couple named Cho, early beneficiaries of the Chinese economic miracle. The Chos designed toys, which were made in their mainland factories and sold worldwide. So successful were they that five years ago they'd bought an estate in rural Massachusetts, less than three hundred miles from either Boston or New York, and now split their time between China and the United States.

Their staff in the Massachusetts house was five Chinese nationals with no English, illegally brought in, mistreated, and paid nothing. The finale came when the Chos' cook died of a burst appendix. The Chos, unwilling to risk exposure by seeking medical assistance, had preferred to believe the cook was malingering and could be cured with a few extra beatings. When they'd tried to bribe a local mortician to keep the death quiet, he instead went to the police.

So now Gwen was here in this stately New England country house filled with bright-colored Oriental decorations, sitting with a woman named Franny from Immigration and a translator named Koh Chi from a nearby community college. The four remaining staff/ slaves, frightened out of their wits, were haltingly telling their stories in Mandarin, while Koh Chi translated and a tape recorder stood witness. The Chos themselves were at the moment in state holding cells, and would be questioned when their attorney arrived from Boston tomorrow.

This particular job was slow and tedious, but also heartbreaking, and Gwen wasn't entirely displeased when the cell phone in her shoulder bag vibrated. Seeing it was her office, she murmured to Franny, "I have to take this," and went out to the hall to answer.

It was Chief Inspector Davies. "Are you very tied up there?"

"Pretty much, sir."

"They found some of the money," he said.

It had been too long. She said, "Money, sir?"

"From the armored car."

"Oh, my gosh! They *found* it?"

"Some of it. Also a body. We're working on ID now."

"I'll be right there," she said, and went back to explain to Franny and to make her promise to send a tape after the interviews.

*   *   *

It was the conference room at the state police barracks this time. In addition to Chief Davies at the head of the table, there were a pair of state troopers sitting along one side, a man and a woman, who introduced themselves as Danny Oleski and Louise Rawburton. Both looked very sheepish. It wasn't a usual thing to see a state trooper look sheepish, so Gwen wondered, as she took a chair across from them, what was going on.

Introductions over, Inspector Davies said, "Let the troopers tell you their story." He himself was looking grim; "hanging judge" was the phrase that came to Gwen's mind.

The troopers glanced at each other, and then the woman, Rawburton, said, "I'll tell it," and turned to Gwen. "Out on Putnam Road," she said, "there's a church called St. Dympna that was shut down some years ago. My family went there when I was a little girl. The week before last, when we were told to forget the roadblocks and concentrate on empty buildings instead, St. Dympna was in our area."

"When we got there," the male trooper, Oleski, said, "two men and a woman were unloading boxes of hymnals from the church into an old Econoline van. It had the name Holy Redeemer Choir on the doors."

"We looked in a couple of the boxes," Rawburton said, "and they were hymnals. When I said I used to go to that church the woman even gave me one of them."

Oleski said, "The minister's house was across the road. Also empty. Upstairs, we found a back window broken out, looked as though it could have been recent. When we went back to our car to report the broken window, the van was gone."

Gwen said, "I think I know where this story is going. You went back to the church. Why was that?"

"We happened to go by it," Rawburton said, "and we didn't go inside last time, and I realized I just wanted to see what it looked like."

Gwen said, "You didn't go in last time?"

Oleski said, "The three people were very open. I looked at license and registration, all fine. One of the men was in the basement when we got there, and he came up and said everything was stripped out down there, appliances and all of that."

"They were happy to have us search," Rawburton said. "They *seemed* happy. There just didn't seem to be any point."

Gwen said to Oleski, "You looked at his license. Remember the name?"

Oleski twisted his face into agonized thought. "I've been going nuts," he said. "It was Irish or Scottish. Mac Something. I just can't remember."

"I Googled Holy Redeemer Choir in Long Island, just now," Rawburton said. "There is no such thing."

"When you went in there today," Gwen said, "what did you find?"

"Three boxes of hymnals on the floor," Oleski said. "But when we opened them, it was all money. And when I opened the basement door, the smell came up."

"It was Dalesia," Davies said. "We've got a positive ID now."

"I keep thinking," Rawburton said, "we should have done more, but *what* more? We checked the driver's ID, the car registration, looked in boxes."

"That you opened?" Gwen asked. "Or that they opened?"

Oleski said, "One I opened, two they opened, the second one when the woman gave Louise the hymnbook."

"That's a nice touch, isn't it?" said Davies, the hanging judge.

Gwen said, "And the two men? Any idea who they were?"

Rawburton, looking and sounding more sheepish than ever, said, "They're the two from the posters."

"But that new one, of the guy that was in the basement," Oleski said, "we didn't get to see that until after we'd met them. And it was a lot closer than the first one."

Gwen shook her head and said to Davies, "Nine days ago. They were here, just the way you said, and so was the money, and nine days ago it all left."

"There's no trail," Davies said.

"When I think how many times," Gwen said, "they just slid right through." The idea she never would be calling Bob Modale over in New York to describe the arrest of John B. Allen and Mac Somebody grated on her, but she'd get over it. "Inspector," she said, "I should get back to my Chinese slaves. At least there, I think I can deliver a happy ending."

FOUR

1

Tuesday afternoon, Parker tried calling the phone number in Corpus Christi that had once belonged to Julius Norte, the ID expert, now dead. Had his business been taken over by somebody else?

No; it was a Chinese restaurant now. And when he looked for Norte's legitimate front business, a print shop called Poco Repro, through information, there was no listing.

So he'd have to start again. The guy who'd given him Norte's name in the first place was an old partner named Ed Mackey, who didn't have a direct number but did have cutouts, where messages could be left. Parker used the name Willis, which Mackey would know, left the gas station phone booth number, and said he could be called there Wednesday morning at eleven.

He was seated in position in the car at that time,

when the phone rang, and got to it before it could ring again. "Yes."

"Mr. Willis." It was Mackey's voice. "I guess you're doing fine."

"I'm all right. How's Brenda?"

"Better than all right. She doesn't want me to take any trips for a while."

"This isn't about that. Remember Julius Norte?"

"Down in Texas? That was a sad story."

"Yeah, it was. I wondered if anybody else you know was in that business?"

"Time for a new wardrobe, huh?" Mackey chuckled. "I wish I could say yes, but I've been making do with the old duds myself."

"Well, that's okay."

"No, wait. Let me ask around, there might be somebody. Why don't I do that, ask some people I know, call you tomorrow afternoon if I've got anything?"

"That would be good."

"If I don't get anything, I won't call."

"No, I know."

"Three o'clock all right?"

"I got another phone thing at three tomorrow. Make it two forty-five."

Again Mackey chuckled, saying, "All at once, you sound like a lawyer. I hope I have reason to call you tomorrow."

"Thanks."

*   *   *

On Thursday afternoon, he was parked beside the phone-on-a-stick a few minutes early. At quarter to three the phone did ring and it was Mackey. "I got a maybe," he said.

"Good."

"It's a friend-of-a-friend kind of thing, so there's no guarantees."

"I got it."

"He's outside Baltimore, the story is he's a portrait painter."

"Okay."

"You call him, it's because you want a picture of yourself or the missus or the dog or the parakeet."

"Uh-huh. What name do I use?"

"Oh, with him? Forbes recommended him, Paul Forbes."

"Okay."

"Here's his cell." Mackey gave him a phone number. "His name, he says his name, is Kazimierz Robbins. Two Bs."

"Kazimierz Robbins."

"I don't know him," Mackey warned. "I only heard he's been around a few years, people seem to trust him."

"Maybe I will, too," Parker said.

*   *   *

"Hell-lo." It was an old man's voice, speaking with a heavy accent, as though he were talking and clearing his throat at the same time.

"Kazimierz Robbins?"

"That's me."

"A friend of mine told me you do portraits."

"From time to time, that's what I do, although I am to some extent retired. Which friend told you about me?"

"Paul Forbes."

"Ah. You want a special portrait."

"Very special."

"Special portraits, you know, are special expensive. Is this a portrait of yourself, or of your wife, or of someone close to you?"

"Me."

"I would have to look at you, you see."

"I know that."

"Are you in Baltimore?"

"No, I'm north of you, but I can get there. You give me an address and a time."

"You understand, my studio is not in my home."

"Okay."

"I use the daylight hours to do my work. Artificial light is no good for realistic painting."

"Okay."

"These clumpers and streakers, they don't care what the color is. But I care."

"That's good."

"So my consultations are at night, not to interfere with my work. I return to my studio to discuss the client's needs. Could you come here tonight?"

"Tomorrow night."

"That is also good. Would nine o'clock be all right for you?"

"Yes."

"Excellent. And when you come here, sir, what is your name?"

"Willis."

"Willis." There was a hint of "v" in the name. "We will see you then, Mr. Willis," he said, and gave the address.

Five minutes later, Parker called Cosmopolitan Beverages and was put through to Meany, who said, "Mr. Albert said, if I want to deal with a son of a bitch like you, it's okay with him."

"Good."

"The price is acceptable, and we'll work out delivery."

"Good."

"One step first."

"What's that?"

"We have to see what we're getting. We need a sample."

"Fine. It's still ten for one."

Meany sounded doubtful. "Meaning?"

"We give you ten K, you give us one K."

Meany laughed. "I love how we trust each other," he said.

"Or," Parker said, "you could just give me your cash, and hope for the best."

"No, we'll do it your way. How do you want to work this?"

"I'm busy the next couple of days," Parker told him. "A guy I know will call and set up the switch."

"I've probably seen this guy."

"Maybe."

"In a red pickup?"

Parker waited.

"Okay," Meany said. "This guy will call me. What's his name?"

Parker thought. "Red," he said.

"Red. I like that. You're easier to deal with," Meany said, "when you're not trying to prove a point."

"Red will call you."

Hanging up, Parker dialed McWhitney's bar, got him, and said, "I'm on a pay phone," and read off the number. Then he hung up.

It was five minutes before the phone here rang. Parker picked up and immediately reeled off Meany's name and phone number, then said, "Ten grand for one. They need a sample, I'm busy, so you work out the switch. Your name is Red." When he hung up, McWhitney hadn't said a word.

2

Before the Massachusetts armored car job went sour, Parker had had clean documents under a couple of names, papers that were good enough to pass through any usual level of inspection. In getting out from under that job, he'd burned through all of his useful identification, and made it very tough to move around. He had to deal with that right now, make it possible to operate in the world.

How much of a problem this lack of identification meant was shown by the fact that Claire had to drive him to Maryland Friday afternoon. With no driver's license and no credit cards, he couldn't rent a car, and if he borrowed hers and drove it himself and something went wrong, it would kill her identity as well.

Early in the evening of Friday they checked into a motel north of Baltimore and had an early dinner, and then she drove him to Robbins' address on Front Street in a very small town called Vista, near Gunpowder Falls State Park. They'd driven several uphill miles of winding road, but if there was a vista it was too dark to see.

The town, when they got there, wasn't much: one crossroads, a church and firehouse, and half a dozen stores, a couple of them out of business. Robbins' building in this commercial row, two stories high and narrow, with large plate-glass windows flanking a glass front door, still bore a wooden sign above the windows reading VISTA HARDWARE. Inside, through the front windows, the interior was brightly lit, but had not been a hardware store for a long time.

Parker said, "You want to come in or wait?"

"Easier if I wait."

She had parked at the curb in front of the place, the only car stopped along here. Getting out to the old uneven slate sidewalk, Parker saw that the interior of the building was now a kind of gallery, a high-ceilinged room with large paintings on both white-painted side walls. In the middle of the room stood a large easel with a good-size canvas on it, in profile to the windows so that the subject couldn't be seen. In front of the canvas, stooped toward it, brush in right hand, was what had to be Robbins, a tall narrow figure dressed in black, head thrust up and forward as he peered at his work. What he most looked like, the thin angular dark figure in the brightly lit room, was a praying mantis.

Parker rapped a knuckle on the glass of the front door. The painter looked this way, tapped his forehead with the handle end of his brush in salute, put the brush down on the tray beneath the canvas, and walked over to unlock and open the door. His walk looked painful, a little crabbed and distorted, but it must have been that way a long time, because he didn't seem to notice.

He pulled the door open, his leathery face welcoming but wary, and said, "Mr. Willis?"

"For now."

He smiled. "Ah, very good. Come in." Then, looking past Parker, he said, "Your companion does not wish to join us?"

"No, she doesn't want to be a distraction."

"Very astute. I find all beautiful women a distraction." Closing the door, he said, "I think you would prefer to call me Robbins. Kazimierz is not easy for an American to pronounce." He gestured toward the rear of the long room, where a couple of easy chairs and small tables made a kind of living room; or a living room set.

As they walked down the long room, on an old floor of wide pine planks, Parker said, "Why didn't you change the first name?"

"Ego," Robbins said, and motioned for Parker to

sit. "Many are Robbins, or my original name, Rudzik, but from earliest childhood Kazimierz has been me." Also sitting, he leaned forward onto his knees, peered at Parker, and said, "Tell me what you can."

"I no longer have an identity," Parker said, "that's safe from the police."

"Fingerprints?"

"If we're at the point of fingerprints," Parker said, "it's already too late. I need papers to keep me from getting that far."

"And how secure must these be?" He gave a little finger wave and said, "What I mean is, you want more than a simple forged driver's license."

"I want to survive a police computer," Parker said. "I don't have a passport; I want one."

"A legitimate passport."

"Everything legitimate."

Robbins leaned back. "Nothing is impossible," he said. "But everything is expensive."

"I know that."

"We are speaking of approximately two hundred thousand dollars."

"I thought it might be around there."

Robbins cocked an eyebrow, watching him. "This number does not bother you."

"No. If you do the job, it's worth it."

"I would need half ahead of time. In cash, of course. All in cash. How soon could you collect it?"

"I brought it with me in the car."

Robbins gave a surprised laugh. "You *are* serious!"

"I'm always serious," Parker told him. "Now you tell me how you're gonna do it."

"Of course." Robbins thought a minute, looking out over his studio. The paintings on the walls, mounted three or four high, were all portraits, some of well-known faces ranging from John Kennedy to Julia Roberts, some of unknown but interesting faces. All were slightly tinged with a kind of darkness, as though some sort of gloom were being hidden within the paint.

Finally, Robbins nodded to himself and said, "You know I come from the East."

"Yes."

"I did this kind of work for the authorities back there," he said. "For many years. False identities, false papers. There was much work of that kind to be done in those days."

"Sure."

"I imagine there is work of that kind to be done in this country as well," Robbins said, and spread his hands in fatalistic acceptance. "But I am a foreigner, and not that much to be trusted. And I am certain there are Americans who can do the same work."

"Sure."

"I still retain many contacts with my former associates, and in fact travel east two or three times a year.

When a change as complete as you need is called for, my old friends are often of assistance."

"Good."

"Yes." Robbins leaned forward, "When my part of the world was the proletarian paradise," he said, "unfortunately, the infant mortality rate was higher than one would prefer. Many children, born around the same time as yourself, are memorialized by nothing more than a birth certificate and a small grave."

"I get that."

"We start with such a birth certificate," Robbins told him. "To explain your lack of accent, we add documentation that your family emigrated, I think to Canada, when you would have been no more than thirteen years of age. Do you know people in Canada?"

"No."

"Unfortunate." Robbins shook his head at the difficulty. "What we must do," he said, "is bring you to this country very recently, so you will be applying for a Social Security card only now."

Parker considered that. "I was the Canadian representative of an American company," he decided.

"You can do that?"

"Yes. I'll have to phone the guy to tell him about it, that's all."

"Good. Do you have an attorney you can trust?"

"I can find one."

"I think," Robbins said, "you changed your name many years ago, when you were first in Canada. Because of your schoolmates, you see. But never officially. So now that you are in the US, you will first go to the court to have your name legally changed from whatever is on that birth certificate to whomever you would rather be than Mr. Willis."

"Go through the court," Parker said.

"If we are going to legitimize you," Robbins said, "we must use as many legitimate means as possible. What state do you live in?"

"New Jersey."

"They process many name changes there," Robbins assured him. "It will not be a problem. So with your birth certificate and your court order for the name change, you will apply for and receive your Social Security card. After that, there is no question. You are who you say you are."

"You make it sound pretty easy," Parker told him.

"And yet, it is not." Robbins' smile, when he showed it, was wintery. Reaching for a yellow legal pad and a ballpoint pen on the table beside himself, he said, "Your employer while you lived in Canada?"

"Cosmopolitan Beverages. They're based in Bayonne, New Jersey."

"And the man there I would talk to? To get some employment documents, you see."

"Frank Meany."

"You have his e-mail address?"

"No, I have his phone number."

"Ah, well, that will do."

Parker gave him the number and, as he wrote it down, Robbins said, "E-mail has the advantage, you see, that it has no accent. The only three things left for right now are the money, and I must take a photograph of you, and you must tell me your choice of a name."

"I'll bring the money in," Parker said, and went outside, where Claire lowered the passenger window so he could lean in and say, "It's gonna be all right. We're still happy with the name?"

"I am. You want the money from the trunk?"

"Yes."

Opening the trunk, he brought out the duffel bag he'd brought down with him from upstate New York and carried it into Vista Hardware, where Robbins had moved to stand beside a refectory table along the right wall, beneath portraits of Kofi Annan and Clint Eastwood. In all the pictures, the eyes were as wary as Robbins' own.

He seemed amused by the duffel bag. "Usually," he said, "people who traffic in large quantities of cash carry briefcases."

"The money's just as good in this."

"Oh, I'm sure it is."

Robbins picked up from the floor under the table

a cardboard carton that had originally contained a New Zealand white wine. "it will be just as good in this as well," he said.

Parker started lifting stacks of currency from the duffel bag. They were both silent as they counted.

3

Driving east across New Jersey on Interstate 80 Monday afternoon, Parker passed a car with the bumper sticker DRIVE IT LIKE YOU STOLE IT, which was exactly what he was doing. On long hauls like last weekend's trip down to Maryland, it would be too risky for him to drive, but for the sixty-mile run across the state from Claire's place to Bayonne there shouldn't be a problem. He held himself at two miles above the speed limit, let most of the other traffic hurry by—including DRIVE IT LIKE YOU STOLE IT—and stayed literally under the radar.

To get to Cosmopolitan Beverages, he had to drop south of the interstates just before the Holland Tunnel, and drive down into what was still called the Port of New York, even though years ago, with the changeover from longshoremen to containers, just about all the port's activity had moved over to the Jersey side of the bay: Newark, Elizabeth, Jersey City, and Bayonne.

Bayonne, being at the southeast edge of northern New Jersey, with Staten Island so close to its southern shore there was a bridge across, was protected from the worst of the Atlantic weather and out of the way of the heaviest of the shipping lanes. This was the home of the legitimate part of Cosmopolitan Beverages, in an area totally industrial, surrounded by piers, warehouses, gasoline storage towers, freight tracks, chainlink fences, and guard shacks. Most of the traffic here was big semi trailers, and most of those were towing the large metal containers that had made this port possible.

In the middle of all this, standing alone on an island of frost-heaved concrete spottily patched with asphalt, stood a broad three-story brick building long ago painted a dull gray. On its roof, in gaudy contrast, a gleaming red-and-gold neon sign proclaimed COSMOPOLITAN in flowing script and, beneath that, BEVERAGES in smaller red block letters.

A chain-link fence stretched across the concrete-and-asphalt area in front of the building, extending back on both sides toward the piers and Upper New York Bay. Gates in both front corners of the fence stood open and unguarded, the one on the left leading to a mostly full parking lot beside the building, the one on the right opening to a smaller space with only two cars in it at the moment, and with a sign on the fence near the gate reading VISITOR PARKING.

Parker turned in there, left the Toyota with the other visiting cars, and followed a concrete walk across the front of the building to the revolving-door entrance. Inside was a broad empty reception area, containing nothing but a wide low black desk on a shiny black floor. Mobbed-up businesses do try to look like normal businesses, but not very hard. It hadn't occurred to anybody there to put visitor seating in the reception area because they really didn't care.

The wall behind the desk was curved and silver, giving a spaceship effect. Mounted on that wall were bottles of the different liquors the company imported, each in its own clear plastic box, with that brand's Christmas gift box next to it.

The man seated at the desk was different from the last time Parker'd been here, a few years ago, but from the same mold; thirties, indolent, uninvolved. The only thing professional about him was his company blazer, maroon with CB in ornate gold letters on the pocket. He was reading a *Maxim* magazine, and he didn't look up when Parker walked over to the desk.

Parker waited, looking down at him, then rapped a knuckle on the shiny black surface of the desk. The guy slowly looked up, as though from sleep. "Yeah?"

"Frank Meany. Tell him Parker's here."

"He isn't in today," the guy said, and looked back at his magazine.

Parker plucked *Maxim* from the guy's hands and tossed it behind him over his shoulder. "Tell him Parker's here."

The guy's first instinct was to jump up and start a fight, but his second instinct, more useful, was to be cautious. He didn't know this jerk who'd just come in and flipped his magazine out of his hands, so he didn't know where in the pecking order he was positioned. The deskman knew he himself was only a peon in the grand scheme of things, somebody's nephew holding down a "job" until his parole was done. So maybe his best move was not to take offense, but to rise above it.

Assuming a bored air, the deskman said, "You can bring back my magazine while I'm calling."

"Sure."

The deskman turned away to his phone console and made a low-voiced call, while Parker watched him. When he hung up, he was sullen, because now he knew Parker was somewhere above him in importance. "You were gonna get my magazine," he said.

"I forgot."

Sorely tried, the deskman got to his feet to retrieve the magazine himself, as a silver door at the far right end of the silver wall opened and another guy in a company blazer came out. This one was older and heavier, with a little more business veneer on him. Holding the doorknob, he said, "Mr. Parker?"

"Right."

Parker followed him through the silver door into another world. Beyond the reception area, the building was strictly a warehouse, long and broad, concrete-floored, with pallets of liquor cartons stacked almost all the way up to the glaring fluorescents just under the ten-foot ceiling. There was so much clatter of machinery, forklifts, cranes, that normal conversation would have been impossible.

Parker followed his guide through this to Meany's office, off to the right, a roomy space but not showy. The guide held the door for Parker, then closed it after him, as Meany got up from his desk and said, "I didn't know you were coming. Sit down over there."

It was a black leather armchair to the right of the desk. Parker went to it and Meany sat again in his own desk chair. Neither offered to shake hands.

Meany said, "What can I do you for today?"

"You liked the sample."

"It's very nice money," Meany said, "Too bad it's radioactive."

"Do you still want to buy the rest of it?"

"If we can work out delivery," Meany said. "I got no more reason to trust you than you got to trust me."

"You could give us reason to trust each other," Parker said.

Meany gave him a sharp look. "Is this something new?"

"Yes. How that money came to me, things went wrong."

Meany's smile was thin, but honestly amused. "I got that idea," he said.

"At the end of it," Parker told him, "my ID was just as radioactive as that money."

"That's too bad," Meany said, not sounding sympathetic. "So you're a guy now can't face a routine traffic stop, is that it?"

"I can't do anything," Parker told him. "I've got to build a whole new deck."

"I don't get why you're telling me all this."

"For years now," Parker told him, "I've been working for your office in Canada."

Meany sat back, ready to enjoy the show. "Oh, yeah? That was you?"

"A guy named Robbins is gonna call you, ask for some employment records. I know you do this kind of thing, you've got zips, you've got different kinds of people your payroll office doesn't know a thing about."

"People come into the country, people go back out of the country," Meany said, and shrugged. "It's a service we perform. They gotta have a good-looking story."

"So do I."

Meany shook his head. "Parker," he said, "why in hell would I do *you* a favor?"

"Ten dollars for one."

Meany looked offended. "That's a deal we got."

"And this is the finder's fee," Parker said, "for bringing you the deal."

Sitting back in his chair, Meany laced his fingers over his chest. "And if I tell you to go fuck yourself?"

"Tell me," Parker said, "you think there's anybody else in this neighborhood does export?"

"You'd walk away from the deal, in other words."

"There's no such thing as a deal," Parker told him. "There never was, anywhere. A deal is what people say is gonna happen. It isn't always what happens."

"You mean we didn't shake hands on it. We didn't do a paper on it."

"No, I mean, so far it didn't happen. If it happens, fine. If it doesn't, I'll make a deal with somebody else, and it'll be the same story. It happens, or it doesn't happen."

"Jesus, Parker," Meany said, shaking his head. "I never thought I'd say this, but you're easier to put up with when you have a gun in your hand."

"A gun is just something that helps make things happen."

"What I don't get," Meany said, "is how this finder's fee that you call it is gonna give us reason to trust each other. That's what you said, right?"

"You're gonna know my new straight name," Parker pointed out. "And how I got it. So then we've both been useful to each other, so we have a little more trust for each other. And I know, if sometime you decide you don't like me, you could wreck me."

"I *don't* like you."

"We'll try to live with that," Parker said.

Meany gave an angry shake of the head, then reached for notepad and pen. "The guy that's gonna call me, he's named Robbins?"

"Kazimierz Robbins."

Meany looked at the notepad and pen. "Robbins will do," he decided.

As Meany wrote, Parker said, "The other thing is the money switch."

Meany put down the pen. "You wouldn't just like to drop it off here."

"No. Tomorrow, at one p.m., one of your guys in the maroon coats drives onto the ferry at Orient Point out on Long Island that goes over the Sound to New London in Connecticut. He's got our money in boxes or bags or whatever you want. On the ferry, he gets out of the car and one of us gets into it. If that doesn't happen, he drives off, turns around, takes the next ferry back. At some point, we'll take the car. He stays on the ferry while it goes back and forth, and after a while the car comes back with the money for you in it, and he takes it and goes."

Meany said, "And what if the car doesn't come back? You've got our money, but we don't have yours."

"Then how do you help me get my new ID? See?" Parker spread his hands. "It's how we build trust," he said.

4

On the way back to Claire's place, Parker stopped at the usual gas station, phoned McWhitney's bar, and when the man came on said, "I'm in a phone booth." When McWhitney called back five minutes later Parker said, "It's worked out with Meany."

"The ferry switch? No snags?"

"Nothing to talk about. I'll have Claire drive me to the city tomorrow morning, and then I'll take the train out to your place."

"Doesn't that get old?"

"Yes. I'm working on that problem, too. I told Meany we'd do the switch around one. You call Sandra."

"Why do we want to bring her in?"

"Because Meany doesn't know her. If they try something after all, she can be useful."

"All right. I suppose it makes sense."

"She can earn her half of Nick. She can come to

Orient Point and take the same ferry as us and not know us."

"I'll see you in the morning," McWhitney said, and hung up.

When he got to Colliver's Pond, the body of water Claire's house was on, he drove past her place and a further mile on around the lake to another seasonal house where he had a stash. More than half of the money in the duffel bag from upstate New York had been spent.

With a green Hefty bag on the seat beside him, he drove back to Claire's house, and as he came down the driveway she stepped out the front door and signaled him not to put the car in the garage. He rolled his window down and she said, "I've been needing the car, I've got some shopping to do."

"We won't have this crap much longer," he said, getting out of the Toyota.

"I know. Don't worry about it."

He carried the Hefty bag through the house into the garage, then didn't feel like being indoors, so went out around the back to the water. There were two Adirondack chairs there, on the concrete jetty beside the boathouse. He sat there and looked out over the lake and didn't see any other people. Three months ago this whole area had been alive with vacationers, but now only the few year-rounders were left, and they were all in their houses.

The strong breeze that ruffled the lake and blew past him had hints of frost in it. It was past five on an early November day, and the light was fading fast. Once these two problems were taken care of, the money and the new identification, it would be time for them to head somewhere south.

He didn't hear the car coming back, but he heard the garage door lift open, and got up to go inside, help her unpack the groceries, and then go sit in the living room while she went to her office to listen to her messages. They'd eat out tonight; when she came back, they'd decide where.

But when she walked into the living room, there was a troubled look on her face. "One's for you."

It was McWhitney. "Evening, Mr. Willis. I hope I'm not interrupting anything. This is Nelson, the bartender from McW, and I'm sorry to have to tell you you left your briefcase here. Your friend Sid found it and turned it over to me. He doesn't want a reward or anything, but he and a few of his pals are waiting around outside to be sure everything's okay. I hope to hear from you soon. I hope there wasn't anything valuable in there."

5

Parker had had enough. But he knew this was exactly the kind of situation that makes an angry man impatient, an impatient man careless, and a careless man a convict. He was angry, but he would control it.

"I'm sorry," he said, "but I got to ask you to drive me to the city."

She gave him a curious look. "But that's the place we went to, isn't it? Where I met Sandra."

"Right."

"But that's out on Long Island."

"I'll take a train."

"You will not," she said. "Come on, let's go."

"One minute," he said, and went through to the pantry, where he took down from a shelf an unopened box of Bisquick. He turned it over and the bottom had been opened and reclosed. He popped it open and shook out, wrapped in a chamois, a Beretta Bobcat in the seven-shot .22, a twelve-ounce pocket automatic, which he put in his right pants pocket, then returned the chamois to the box and the box to the shelf.

Claire had her coat on, standing by the door between kitchen and garage. Parker chose a loose dark car coat with several roomy pockets, and transferred the Bobcat to one of them. "Ready."

As they went out to the car, she said, "You can tell me what this is along the way."

"I will."

He waited till they were away from the house, then said, "This is about doing something with that money."

"Overseas. You told me."

"That's right. On his own, Nels talked to a guy he knew that could maybe do that, but Nels didn't know him as well as he thought."

"Is this Sid?"

"You mean Nels's message just now. The guy's name is Oscar Sidd. I've never seen him, but he's been described to me. It turned out, when Nels went up to New England to get the money, Oscar Sidd followed him."

"To see if he could get it all for himself."

"That's right. Sandra saw what he was up to, and cut him out of the play."

"But now he's back," Claire said.

"He has to know the money's somewhere around Nels. So what Nels was saying is, Oscar Sidd's outside the bar with some friends of his, or some muscle he bought. To keep things quiet, he's waiting out there until the other customers leave. Then they'll go in and ask Nels where the money is. They'll have plenty of time to ask."

Claire nodded, watching the road. Full night was here now, oncoming traffic dimming its lights. "When will the customers leave?"

"On a Monday night in November? No later than nine o'clock."

She looked at the dashboard clock, "It's five-thirty."

"We'll get there."

"Not if you take a train."

"Nels will hold them off for a while. It won't be that sudden."

"That's why I'll drive you there."

"You don't want to be at that bar, not tonight. Or anywhere near it. Let me off a block away."

"Fine. I can do that."

"And don't wait for me, Nels and I were going to make the money transfer tomorrow anyway. So you just let me off and go back."

"I might stay in the city. Have dinner and go to a late show."

"Good idea."

"And if anything comes up, call me on my cell." She looked at him and away, "All right?"

"Sure," he said.

6

At eight thirty-five on this Monday night McW was the only establishment showing lights along this secondary commercial street in Bay Shore. Parker walked down the block toward the place, seeing a half dozen cars parked along both sidewalks, including, across the way and a little beyond McW, a black Chevy Tahoe parked some distance from the two nearest streetlights. There were some people sitting in the Tahoe, impossible to say how many.

The simplest thing for the problem at hand—and for the anger—would be to go over there and put the Bobcat to work, starting with the driver. But it was better to wait, to take it slow.

To begin with, the people in the Tahoe wouldn't be likely to let somebody just come walking across the street toward them with his hand in his pocket. And he didn't know what the situation was right now inside the bar. So he barely looked over at the Tahoe, but instead walked steadily on, both hands in his pockets, then turned in at McW.

Other than McWhitney, there were four men in the bar. On two stools toward the rear were a pair of fortyish guys in baseball caps, unzipped vinyl jackets, baggy jeans with streaks of plaster dust, and paint-streaked work boots; construction men extending the after-work beer a little too long, by the slow-motion way they talked and lifted their glasses and nodded their heads.

Closer along the bar was an older man in a snap-brim hat and light gray topcoat over a dark suit, with a small pepper-and-salt dog curled up asleep under the stool beneath him as he nursed a bronze-colored mixed drink in a short squat glass and slowly read the *New York Sun*; a dog walker with an evening to kill.

And on the other side, at a booth near the front, facing the door, sat a bulky guy in a black raincoat over a tweed sports jacket and blue turtleneck sweater, a tall glass of clear liquid and ice cubes on the table in front of him. This last one looked at Parker when he walked in, and then didn't look at him, or at anything else.

"I'll take a beer, Nels," Parker called, and angled over to sit at the club-soda-drinker's table, facing him. "Whadaya say?"

"What?" The guy was offended. "Who the hell are you?"

"Another friend of Oscar."

The guy stiffened, but then shook his head. "I don't know Oscar, and I don't know you."

Parker took the Bobcat from his pocket and put it on the table, then left it there with his hands resting on the tabletop to both sides, not too close, "That's who I am," he said. "You Oscar's brother?"

The guy stared at the gun, not afraid of it, but as though waiting to see it move. "No," he said, not looking up. "I got no brothers named Oscar."

"Well, how important is Oscar to you, then? Important enough to die for?"

Now the guy did meet Parker's eyes, and his own were scornful. "The only thing you're gonna shoot off in here is your mouth," he said. "You don't want a lotta noise to wake the dog."

Parker picked up the Bobcat and pushed its barrel into the guy's sternum, just below the rib cage. "In my experience," he said, "with a little gun like this, a body like yours makes a pretty good silencer."

The guy had tried to shrink back when the Bobcat lunged at him, but was held by the wooden back of the booth. His hands shot up and to the sides, afraid to come closer to the gun. He stared at Parker, disbelieving and believing both at once.

McWhitney arrived, with a draft beer he put on

the table out of the way of them both as he said, calmly, "How we doing, gents?"

"Barman," Parker said, keeping his eyes on the guy's face and the Bobcat in his sternum, "reach inside my pal there and take out his piece."

"You cocksucker," the guy said, "you got no idea what's gonna hit you." He glowered at Parker as McWhitney reached inside his coat and drew out a Glock 31 automatic in .357 caliber, a more serious machine than the Bobcat.

"Put it on the table," Parker said. "And your towel," meaning the thin white towel McWhitney carried looped into his apron string.

McWhitney draped the towel on top of the Glock. "What now?"

"Our friend," Parker said, "is gonna move to the last booth, and sit facing the other way. He does anything else, I kill him. And you bring him a real drink."

"I will."

Parker brought the Bobcat back and put it in his pocket, his other hand on the towel on the Glock. To the guy he said, "Up," and when the guy, enraged but silent, got to his feet, Parker said, "You got anything on your ankles?"

"No." The guy lifted his pants legs, showing no ankle holsters. Bitterly, he said, "I wish I did."

"No, you don't. Go."

The guy walked heavily away down the bar, working his shoulder muscles as though in preparation for a fistfight.

Parker said to McWhitney, "Time to close the place."

"Right."

McWhitney went away behind the bar again and Parker put the Glock and the towel in another of his pockets. He closed a hand around his beer glass but didn't drink, and McWhitney called, "Listen, guys, time to drink up. I gotta close the joint now."

The customers were good about it. The two construction guys expressed great surprise at how late it was, and comic worry about how their wives would take it. Livelier and more awake once they were on their feet, each assured the other they would certainly tell the wife it was the other guy's fault.

The newspaper reader simply folded his paper and stuffed it into a pocket, got to his feet, picked up his dog's leash, and said, "Night, Nels. Thank you."

"Any time, Bill. Night, guys."

Down at the rear, the bulky guy's back was to the room, as he'd been instructed. Quietly the newspaper reader and more loudly the construction men left the place, Parker trailing after. All called good night again through the open door.

The other three all went off to the left, the dog walker more briskly, his dog trotting along beside him, the construction men joking as they went, weaving a little. Parker angled rightward across the street, then down that sidewalk past the Tahoe, hands in his pockets.

When he was a few paces beyond the Tahoe, he heard its doors begin to open. He turned, taking the Glock and the towel from his pocket, and three men were coming out of the Tahoe, both sides in front and the sidewalk right side in back. All were concentrating on what was in front of them, not what was behind them.

The guy from the front passenger seat was tall and skinny, to match the description of Oscar Sidd. He shut his door and took one pace forward toward the front of the car when Parker shot him, holding the Glock straight-armed inside the towel.

Sidd dropped and the other two spun around, astonished. Parker held the Glock in the towel at waist height, pointed away to the right, and called, "Anybody else?"

The two stared at him, then across the Tahoe roof at each other. The guy on the street side couldn't see Oscar. The other one looked down at the body, looked at his partner, and shook his head.

The driver jumped behind the wheel and the other one into the backseat. The engine roared and the lights flashed on, showing the Tahoe had dealer plates. The driver at first accelerated too hard, so that the wheels spun and smoked, but then he got under control and the Tahoe hurried away from there.

Parker carried the Glock and the towel back into the bar. The bulky guy was still in position in the rear booth. Parker called to him, "Come here," and the guy, sullen-faced, came down along the bar to stand in front of him, look at the Glock, and say, "Yeah?"

"I hope you got your own car here."

The guy frowned at the front door. "Where are they?"

"Gone. Except for Oscar. He's dead out there. He was shot with this gun of yours." Putting it on the bar, Parker said, "Hold on to it, Nels."

"Will do."

Parker looked at the guy. "Did somebody hear me fire one shot? I don't know. Did somebody call the cops? I don't know. Will Oscar be there when they get here? That's up to you."

"Jesus Christ," the guy said, and it was equal parts curse and prayer. He hurried out the door and Parker said to McWhitney, "Let me use your phone."

"Sure."

Parker called Claire's cell phone. "Are you still on the Island?"

"Yes. Are you finished already?"

"Come back, we'll get dinner around here somewhere together—"

"I'll tell you where," McWhitney said.

"—and spend the night down here, and then you
go home tomorrow and I'll come back to Nels."

"What happened?" she said.

"I'm not angry any more," he said.

7

The sign in the window of the door at McW read CLOSED at nine-thirty the next morning, and the green shade was pulled down over the glass, but the door was unlocked. Parker went in and McWhitney was seated at the first booth on the left, drinking a cup of coffee and reading the *Daily News*. He looked up when Parker walked in and said, "Claire get off?"

Parker sat on a stool with his back against the wood of the bar. "Yes."

McWhitney nodded at the wall above the backbar, where a television set on a shelf was switched on with the sound turned off. "There's news on the news."

"For us?"

"They found Nick's body."

Parker shrugged. "Well, that's all right."

"You want coffee, by the way?"

"No, Claire and I ate."

"Well, maybe the Nick thing is all right and maybe it isn't." McWhitney waggled his palm over the newspaper, to indicate the question.

Parker said, "Why wouldn't it be all right? We're done up there."

"The hymnbooks," McWhitney said. "I was gonna drop them off at a church around here. Just to get rid of them, but now I don't know. Can they be traced back to the church up there? I don't want anything anywhere around me that hooks to anything in Massachusetts."

"We'll dump them somewhere else," Parker said.

McWhitney shook his head, "I never thought I'd sit around," he said, "and try to figure out what to do to get rid of a load of hot hymnbooks."

"The money's mostly what we have to deal with," Parker said. "Make the load lighter. Hefty bags are good for that."

"Maybe three of them. It's a lot of cash."

"Where's the truck?"

"In an open parking lot a couple blocks from here. I figured," McWhitney said, "a piece of crap like that little truck, if we give it a lotta security, it'll look like something might be inside there."

"Hymnbooks."

"Right." McWhitney yawned and pushed the *News* away from himself, "I talked on the phone with Sandra this morning," he said. "She checked the ferry on the

Web. The one we want's at one o'clock. Takes an hour and twenty minutes, we come back on the three."

"Fine," Parker said. "But now I'm thinking about another complication from Nick."

McWhitney laughed. "That Nick," he said. "He's one complication after another, isn't he? What now?"

"The troopers that stopped by when we were unloading the boxes out of the church," Parker said.

"Sure. The woman went to that church when she was a little kid."

"And now they found Nick," Parker said. "Do they start to wonder about that truck?"

"Well, shit," McWhitney said.

"They didn't write anything down," Parker said. "They looked at your license but they didn't do anything about it."

"No, that's right."

"But they're going to remember those words on the door. Holy Redeemer Choir."

"And they'll look here, and they'll look there, and they won't *find* any Holy Redeemer Choir."

"At least, not the same one."

McWhitney looked bleak. "And we're gonna take that same truck on a ferry to New England."

"That place where you had the name painted on," Parker said, "is he around here?"

"Yeah, walking distance. In fact, I walked it."

"Could he paint the name out again?"

Getting up from the booth, McWhitney said, "Let me call him, I mean, why not?"

"We should have just time before we have to go get the ferry. And if not, we'll get the next ferry."

Walking around the end of the bar to the phone, McWhitney said, "When this is over, I'm gonna be nothing but a bartender for a long long time to come."

8

On the phone the car painter told McWhitney he could do a quick spray job of the body color over the names on the doors in five minutes, so he and Parker walked to the parking lot where McWhitney had left the truck. Along the way, Parker said, "The only thing we've got to do today is the money switch, get that stuff out of our hands. The hymnbooks is something for later."

"I don't like it," McWhitney said, "but I know you're right."

"Where's your pickup?"

"Behind my place. If there was room, I'd have put the truck back there, too, but it's too tight."

"We'll switch the boxes of books to the pickup," Parker said, "then take care of the money."

"Okay, fine."

Along their walk they came to a deli, where Parker bought a box of ten large Hefty bags. Then they went on to reclaim the van and drive it the four blocks to the body shop and auto paint place, a sprawling low dark-brick building taking up most of this industrial block. The closed garage door in the middle of the otherwise blank wall had a big sign, red letters on white, HONK, so McWhitney honked, and in a minute a smaller door that was part of the garage door opened and a guy in coveralls looked out.

McWhitney called, "Tell George it's Nelson," and the guy nodded and went back inside, shutting the door.

They waited another two or three minutes, and then the full garage door lifted and another guy in coveralls came out, this one also wearing a baseball cap, black-framed eyeglasses, and a thick black moustache. He came over to McWhitney at the wheel of the van, grinned at him, grinned at the name on the door, and said, "Well, it looks like you got religion and then you lost it again."

"That's about it."

"It's a quick job, but I need to do it inside, I need the compressor."

"Sure."

George leaned closer to McWhitney's window, "The job may be quick," he said, with a friendly smile, "but it isn't cheap."

McWhitney slid a hundred-dollar bill from his shirt pocket, and extended it, palm down, toward George, saying, "A quick job like this, it doesn't even have to show up in the cash register."

"That's very true," George said, and made the hundred disappear. "You can both stay in the car," he said. "Follow me." And he turned away, walking back into the building, McWhitney following.

Inside, the building was mostly one broad open space, concrete-floored, full of racket. Auto-body parts were being pounded or painted, other parts were being moved on metal-wheeled dollies over the concrete floor, and at least two portable radios were playing different ideas about music. A couple of dozen men were working in here, all of them in coveralls, most of them either shouting or singing.

There was no way to have a conversation in here, not once you got half a dozen feet in from the door. George directed them with hand gestures. While the first guy shut the door behind them, George guided them on a path through automobiles, automobile parts, and machinery to a large oblong cleared area with a big rectangular metal grid suspended above it. From the grid, large shiny metal ductwork extended up to the ceiling.

George had McWhitney park directly beneath the grid, then went away and the loud whine of an air compressor joined the mix of noise. George came up the left side of the van from behind, carrying a spray gun attached to a black rubber hose, and hunkered down beside McWhitney's door. The whining went to a higher pitch, then lower again, and George walked his spray gun and hose back down the left side and up the right side to do the same to the other door. He stepped back, looked at his work, nodded to himself, and carried the spray gun away again.

When he next came into view, he motioned to them to follow him, and McWhitney steered the van along more lanes through the work to a different garage door that opened onto the side street. They drove out and stopped on the sidewalk, so both Parker and McWhitney could get out and look at the doors.

The words were gone, without a trace. The fresh paint was darker and shinier than the rest, but nevertheless the same color.

George, standing beside McWhitney to look at his work, said, "It'll dry pretty fast, and then it'll be the same color as the body."

"Good."

"Being out here and not in the shop, it'll get some dust and dirt on it, so it won't be as perfect as it might be. You'll get some little roughness."

"George," McWhitney said, "that really doesn't matter. This is fine."

"I thought so," George said. He was still happy. "Any time we can be of service," he said, "just give us a call."

9

The alley beside McW led to a small bare area behind the building, paved long ago with irregular slabs of slate. The area was confined by the rear of McWhitney's building, the flank of the building next door across the alley, and by two eight-foot-high brick walls on the other two sides. The local building code required two exits from any commercial establishment, and in McW's case the second exit was through the door that led to this area from the bedroom of McWhitney's apartment behind the bar. The space was large enough for McWhitney to park his pickup back there and K-turn himself out again, but not much more.

Now McWhitney backed the van down the narrow alley until he was past his building, with the pickup in the clear area to the left. He and Parker got out of the van, McWhitney backed the pickup closer to the van's rear doors, and they started emptying the van.

The first boxes out were filled with hymnals, heavy but not awkward to move. Then there were the money boxes.

The money inside the boxes was all banded into stacks of fifty bills, always of the same denomination. The bands, two-inch-wide strips of pale yellow paper, were marked DEER HILL BANK, DEER HILL, MA. The stacks made a tight fit inside the boxes.

It turned out to be easiest to dump a box over, empty the money onto the floor of the van, and then stuff it all into the Hefty bags. The emptied box, with its cover restored, would be stacked with the others in the bed of the pickup.

As they worked, McWhitney said, "It's a pity about this stuff. Look how beautiful it is."

"It'll tempt you," Parker said. "But it's got a disease."

"Oh, I know."

When they were finished, the pickup, sagging a bit, was crammed with boxes, empty and full, and three roundly stuffed Hefty bags squatted in the back of the van. McWhitney looked at his watch. "My barman'll be here in fifteen minutes," he said, "and then we can take off. Come on inside."

To obey the fire code, the door at the back of his building had to be openable from inside at all times during business hours, but from outside it took a key to get in. McWhitney unlocked the door and they went through his small but neat living quarters to the bar, where McWhitney said, "You want a beer for the road?"

"Later."

"I don't trust later, I'll take mine now. You want to call Sandra?"

"Sure. Give me the phone."

McWhitney slid the phone across the bar to Parker, drew himself a draft, and watched the conversation.

"Keenan."

"Hello, Sandra."

"I'm on my way," she said. "I think I should be there ahead of everybody so I can see if anybody has extra company."

"Good idea. We'll be in the same van, but it doesn't have any words on it any more."

"Oh, you got the news. If that cop didn't have her girlish memories of that church, she wouldn't have any reason to remember us *or* the van."

"Well, it doesn't matter any more. See you later."

Parker hung up, and McWhitney said, "What doesn't matter any more?"

"The cops at the church."

"I don't intend to drive through their territory for quite a while," McWhitney said, and opened the drawer in the backbar beneath the cash register. "This piece we took from the fella last night," he said. "I don't feel like I want it in my joint any more, and on the other hand, where we're going, what we're doing, it might not be a bad idea to bring along an extra gun."

"Sure. Bring it."

McWhitney tried to stuff it into the inside pocket of his jacket, but it was too large and too heavy. "I'll carry it in the glove compartment," he decided. "Then drop it off the ferry. If things are going well."

10

From where they were in Bay Shore on the south shore of Long Island, it was about seventy miles to the Orient Point ferry farther east and up on the north shore. Half of that trip was on highway, starting with the Sagtikos Parkway north, and then the Long Island Expressway east, but at Riverhead the Expressway, which had been getting thinner and thinner of traffic, ran out and from there they were on smaller roads on this less populated end of the island, with the ferry terminal still thirty-five miles ahead.

They'd been driving beyond the Expressway for about five minutes, first on Edwards Avenue north almost to Long Island Sound, and then east on Sound Avenue, when McWhitney, looking alert, said, "Yeah?" He cocked his head, listening, and Parker knew Sandra was calling him on his hands-free phone. Around them now was mostly sand and scruffy wasteland, with a mix of small homes and businesses, some of them already shut for the season.

"Sure," McWhitney told the space in front of him, and took his foot off the accelerator. The van dropped about ten miles an hour in speed, and then he tapped the accelerator again, maintaining that new speed, for two or three minutes.

Parker watched and waited, not wanting to interrupt if Sandra had anything else to say, and then McWhitney said, "Okay, got it. Let me know if they do anything else."

Parker said, "Somebody following us?"

"A black Chevy Suburban with dealer plates," McWhitney said. "Whatever speed I like, he likes." Gradually he was accelerating back up to his previous speed.

"The car Sidd and the others had last night," Parker said, "was also a Chevy with dealer plates. This is Sidd's pals."

McWhitney grinned. "They got a friend in the car business."

"They came along after us," Parker said, "because they wanted to know where we were going."

"Then they've pretty well got it figured out by now," McWhitney said. "Once you get out here past Riverhead, there's only three things you can do. Take the ferry, swim, or turn around."

"The question is," Parker said, "do we take them out, or do we ignore them?"

"It's a public highway in the middle of the day," McWhitney said. "Not a lot of traffic, but there's *some*. It just makes more trouble to try to deal with them. And they're not gonna want to try to mess with us either, not while we're moving out here in the daylight."

"What about on the ferry?"

"No privacy." McWhitney shrugged, "I'll stay with the van. There's other people gonna stay in their cars, not go upstairs. They read their paper, do some work, I won't be alone. You go find the blazer and get his keys."

"A time is gonna come," Parker said, "when we'll have to deal with those people."

"That's the time," McWhitney said, "they'll be delivered into our hands. What?"

That last wasn't directed to Parker, but to the voice in his ear, because after listening McWhitney laughed and said, "That's very nice. You just make it up as you go along."

Parker said, "She's gonna move on them?" He didn't like that idea. It would be better if they didn't know about Sandra until and unless she was really needed.

But McWhitney said, "No. She wanted me to slow

down again because she's gonna accelerate out ahead of them to be in front when they board."

Parker nodded. "That's good."

"Then," McWhitney said, "we'll see what trouble she can make." Again he laughed. "I bet she can make a little," he said.

11

At the ferry terminal, a large flat open space at the end of the North Fork of Long Island, facing south though the ferry would travel north, the drivers first paid their fares, and then the cars were lined up in rows on a large parking area with lanes painted on it. There they would wait for the southbound ferry to come in and unload its group of cars and foot passengers, before they'd be boarded in the order in which they'd arrived.

The van's position was halfway down the third occupied lane. That lane filled up pretty fast, and then more cars came down on the right beside them, filling in the next lane. Out in the water, the large white-and-blue ferry could be seen slowly maneuvering itself toward the dock.

Into a silence, in the van, McWhitney suddenly said,

"What?" Then, to Parker, he said, "She says to look over our shoulder."

Parker tried to look back through the van's rear window, but there was nothing to see except the front of the car tucked in close behind them. So he bent to the side until he could look in his outside mirror, and there, two cars behind them, was Sandra's black Honda with its whip antennas. Behind it he could just see a black Chevy Suburban.

"She's back there and so are they," he said.

"I hate to be followed," McWhitney said. "It makes me antsy."

"We'll tell them," Parker said.

It was about fifteen minutes more before the ferry was loaded for the trip to Connecticut. Once everybody was aboard and the ferry was moving out of its slip into Gardiner's Bay, Parker said, "I'll find the guy now."

"I'm keeping the doors locked," McWhitney said. "No point being *too* carefree."

Parker got out of the van and McWhitney clicked the door locked behind him. He made his way up the metal stairs to the upper deck, where there were lines at the refreshment stand. Big windows looked out onto the view of sea and sky, and there was bench seating both inside and out.

Parker didn't see the bulky guy from last night, and he didn't see Sandra, but looking through a side window he saw a maroon blazer out there, the guy strolling along the rail. When he stepped out, it was the same guy who'd led him back to Meany's office at Cosmopolitan Beverages last week.

Parker said, "So here we are."

"Here we are," the guy agreed. Out here, he was smiling, relaxed. "I want to thank you," he said. "You got me a day off and a nice jaunt on the ocean."

"That's fine," Parker said, and looked around. He still didn't see anybody else he knew.

The guy picked up on his tension. "Everything okay? Is it all right to give you the keys?"

"Yeah. Do it now."

The guy pulled keys from his pocket and handed them to Parker, saying, "About the middle, on the left. It's a Subaru Forester, green. Anything I should know about?"

"No. A couple of people are trying to deal themselves in. We'll take care of it."

"Frank would like his car back," the guy said, and grinned again, this grin a little less relaxed. "And the other, too, of course."

"It's taken care of," Parker said. "I gotta go. If they see me talking to you, they say, who's that?"

The guy's grin this time was self-confident. "They don't wanna know."

"Hold the thought," Parker said, and went back inside.

Now he saw the bulky guy from last night, on line at the refreshment stand. Parker skirted the line without being seen, went on down to the cars, found the Forester, and unlocked his way in. On the backseat were two liquor cartons. He didn't bother to look in them.

From here, the Chevy Suburban was almost parallel to him, two cars over, with Sandra's Honda in front of it, and McWhitney in the van closer to the front of the ship. Parker put the key in the ignition, and waited.

There was a glitch in unloading the ferry in New London. The first cars got off all right, including McWhitney in the van, but then Sandra couldn't seem to start the Honda. She ground the starter, and people behind her began to honk and shout and get out of their vehicles. Other lines of cars moved, but that one was stuck. When Parker drove off, the bulky guy and one other from the Suburban were pushing the Honda.

McWhitney had waited beside the road. He was laughing when Parker went by, and rolled in to follow him. They drove into town, found a supermarket, and Parker went to the rear of its parking lot. McWhitney stopped next to him, still laughing, and got out of the van to say, "She got them to help. You believe the balls on that woman?"

"Let's do this fast," Parker said. "We've got half an hour before the ferry goes back."

As they started the transfer of the three Hefty bags and the two liquor cartons, McWhitney said, "I've been thinking about this. We're still gonna have money in this van. Not the dirty two mil, the clean two hundred K."

"That's right," Parker said.

"So they'll still have something to go after," McWhitney said. "So what I think, I don't take the ferry back. You do and Sandra does, you give the beverage guy this Subaru and you travel with Sandra, come back together to my place."

"It'll take you five hours to come around," Parker said, "Almost all the way back to the city, and then out onto the Island."

"But they know this van," McWhitney said, "And we rubbed their noses in it pretty good last night, so now they got an extra motivation. You know I'm not gonna skip out on you because I'm not gonna skip out on my bar. You'll be there by five-thirty, I'll be there by eight. And Sandra can keep in touch with me."

"All right," Parker said. "I'll see you there."

12

It was a shorter wait this time for Parker to board the ferry, driving the Forester up the ramp, following the hand signals of the ferry crew, coming to a stop very near the front of the boat. The three large Hefty bags filled most of the space behind him, one on the rear seat and two squeezed into the cargo area.

Once again he waited for the ferry to move away from the land and make its turn before he got out of the Forester, locked it, and headed for the stairs. He didn't look for Sandra's Honda yet, but would find it when he needed it.

Frank Meany's man was promenading on the same side deck as last time. He looked relaxed enough to retire. Seeing Parker, he smiled and said, "Everything all right, your end?"

Handing him the car keys, Parker said, "About all

you're going to see in your rearview mirror is Hefty bags."

"Frank loves Hefty bags," the guy said. "Nice to see you again."

Parker went back inside, and saw Sandra coming up the stairs. He went over to her and said, "I'm traveling with you."

"Not yet," she said. "I'm here for the ladies'. I'll be right back."

She went on to the restrooms, and Parker waited near a window in a spot where people coming up the stairs would face the other way. But none of the trio from the Suburban came up, and a few minutes later Sandra returned, waved to Parker, and the two of them went down the stairs to the cars, he saying, "Nelson didn't like bringing the good money back on the boat with those other guys around, so he's gonna drive."

"That'll take him forever."

"He figures to get to his place by eight. We'll wait for him there."

"Okay, good," she said, and pointed. "I'm over this way."

"I'm not seeing the Suburban," he said.

"What?" She looked around. "Oh, for Christ's sake. They've gotta be here."

"You go that way, I'll go this way, but I don't think so."

They moved among the cars and met at the Honda. Looking across it at him, she said, "What are we gonna do?"

"First we get in the car."

She unlocked them in, and when both doors were shut he said, "Call Nelson."

"I can't," she said. "With the steel hull on this thing, I get no reception."

"Go out on a deck."

"It's still no good."

Parker looked at her. "You can't call Nels till we get to Long Island?"

"I hate it as bad as you do," she said.

He shook his head. "Over an hour before we can call him."

"He'll be all right," she said. "He's a big boy."

"Yeah, he is," Parker said. "And they're three big boys."

At Orient Point, once they were off the ferry, Sandra pulled onto the verge of the road, out of the flow of debarking cars, and called McWhitney. Parker watched her face, and saw that McWhitney wasn't picking up.

Then she said, "I'm getting his voice mail. What the fuck, I might as well leave a message. Nelson, call me." She broke the connection and said, "Shit. I needed that money."

"They're still out there," Parker said. "They haven't gone to ground anywhere, not yet. They've got to come back to the Island. If nothing else, they've got to give the car back." Looking out the windshield, he said, "If we knew what the dealer was, we could be waiting for them."

"Oh, well, I can do *that* part," she said.

"You can?"

She gestured to the notepad she kept mounted on the top of the dashboard. "Any car I'm following, or I'm interested in, every time, I write down their plate number."

Parker looked at it. "And you can get the dealer from that?"

"Sure, Keenan and I always cultivated cash-only friendships at the DMV. Hold on."

From her bulky purse she drew a slender black book, opened it, and dialed a number. "Hi. Is Matt Devereaux there? Thanks."

She waited. Beside them, the last of the cars from the ferry were trickling by.

"Hello? Hey, Matt, it's Sandra Loscalzo, how you doing? Well, I've got a cute one here, if you could help me. It's a dealer's plate, so I'm not talking about the car this time, I'm talking about the dealer. Sure." She reeled off the number, then also gave him her cell number, and hung up.

"He'll call back in five minutes," she said, and put

the Honda in gear. "We might as well start. Wherever the dealer is, he isn't gonna be this far out on the Island."

Matt did call her back in five minutes, while they were still in the cluster of traffic from that ferry, everybody westbound on Route 25. "Keenan. Hey, Matt. That's terrific. Say again."

She nudged Parker and pointed at the pad on the dashboard. He picked up the small magnetized pen she kept there, and she said, "DiRienzo Chevrolet, Long Island Avenue, Deer Park." She spelled "DiRienzo," then said, "Thanks, Matt. I'll catch up with you later. Roy? I haven't seen him for a while." Breaking the connection, she said, "Well, that's true. Deer Park's just a little beyond Bay Shore. Any point going there now?"

"Every point," Parker said, "but not yet. We'll go to that neighborhood, find a diner, get something to eat, get in position before eight."

"What if they don't bring it back till tomorrow?"

"They don't want it any more," Parker said, "and their friend at the dealer's gonna get nervous if it stays out overnight."

Sandra frowned out at the slow-moving traffic all around them. They wouldn't get clear of this herd from the ferry for another half hour or more, when they reached the beginning of the Expressway. "You're a strange guy to partner with," she said.

"So are you."

"Do me a favor. Don't kill anybody."

"We'll see," he said.

13

Half a dozen car dealers were clustered along both sides of the wide road in this neighborhood, all of them proclaiming, either by banner or by neon sign, OPEN TIL 9! All the dealerships were lit up like football stadiums, and in that glare the sheets of glass and chrome they featured all sparkled like treasure chests. This was the heart of car country, servicing the after-work automotive needs of the bedroom communities.

At seven thirty-five, when Sandra drove down the road to see DiRIENZO writ large in neon on their side, she said, "What do you want to do?"

"Pull in. We'll look at cars."

There were three separate areas for cars at the DiRienzo lot: new, used, and the customers'. Sandra followed the signs and put the Honda in with the customer cars, then said, "Now I'm shopping with you. I need this to come to an end."

He shook his head and got out, and she followed suit, and immediately a short clean young fellow in suit and tie appeared, smiled a greeting, and said, "You folks looking for a family sedan?"

Sandra's smile was sweeter than his. "We're just looking around."

"Go right ahead," he said, with a sweeping arm gesture that offered them the whole place.

"Thank you."

"I'm Tim, I work here." He produced a business card, which he handed to Sandra, who took it. "Take your time. If I can help you with anything, I'm right here."

"Thank you."

They walked away from him, and Sandra said, "Do we want a new family sedan or a used family sedan?"

"We want to get over near the building. I need to see how they're going to come in, what they'll do."

The building was broad, one tall story high, the front mostly wide expanses of plate glass, the rest a neutral gray concrete. A few of the most special cars were given their own spaces on the gleaming floor of the inside showroom, with desks and cubicles and closed-off offices behind. On the right side of the building, farther back than the plate glass, the gray concrete wall continued, with three large overhead doors spaced along the way, all of them at the moment shut.

Parker and Sandra saw that, then moved on past the

front of the building, Parker saying, "They'll bring it in there, by the doors. Their own car will be back with the customer parking. We'll see what happens when they make the transfer."

"We've got at least half an hour to wait," she said. "What do we do in the meantime?"

"Look at cars."

It was more like fifty minutes, and twice in that time they could see the fellow who'd first greeted them look over in their direction, frowning. But he never quite made the move to find out what they were up to.

Sandra said, "Is that it?"

It was. They were walking among the new cars, and the Suburban had to circle around that area to get to the side entrances. They angled to move toward where it would finish up, and as it drove by them Sandra said, "That's weird."

Parker had been looking the other way, not wanting the bulky guy from last night to see and recognize him, but now he turned back, watched the Suburban move slowly among the cars and customers, and said, "What's weird?"

"Only the driver in front, three others in back. What would they do that for?"

Ahead, the Suburban made the turn to go around the corner of the building, putting itself into profile, and Parker could see the middle man of the three in back. "It's Nelson," he said.

"My God," she said, staring, "it is! Did he go over to them?"

"No."

"Well, why lug him around?"

The Suburban stopped in front of the middle overhead door as another suited salesman, a little older, smiling broadly and making gestures of greeting, came around toward it from the front entrance. The driver stepped out to the macadam. The three in the backseat stayed in the car.

"I'll tell you why," Parker said. "Oscar Sidd told them it was going to be two million dollars of poisoned money. They opened the boxes and they only found two hundred thousand. They think it's the same money, and they want to know where the rest of it is."

Sandra stared toward McWhitney. "He's their prisoner in there."

"And that's why he's alive."

Across the way, the driver and the salesman had shaken hands, and now the driver was explaining something. The salesman looked toward the Suburban's backseat, then bowed his head and seriously listened. The driver, finished, patted his arm and walked away toward the customer parking area. The salesman stood waiting, hands clasped in front of himself, like an usher at a wedding.

Parker, watching the Suburban, said, "Go get your car, bring it here."

"I'm better as a spectator," she said, "than a participant."

"Not this time. Do it."

She went away and the salesman conferred with a guy in work clothes, who'd come out a side door and who now bent down to start removing the front license plate.

Now a white Buick Terrazza came out of customer parking and angled over to stop beside the Suburban. Parker moved in closer as the two in back, one of them the bulky guy from last night, hustled McWhitney out of the backseat of the Suburban, wanting to move him quickly and smoothly across to the backseat of the Terrazza.

It didn't happen. Because there were so many other people around, and so much bright light was shining down, they couldn't grasp him as they might have liked. In that instant when all three men were between cars, the two on the outside crowding McWhitney but not quite touching him, he suddenly swept his bent left arm up and back, the elbow smashing into the cheek of the guy on that side, who staggered back into the side of the Suburban and slid sideways to the ground, unmoving.

While the bulky guy on the right was still figuring out a reaction, McWhitney used the same cocked left arm to drive a straight hook into his face, while his right hand lunged inside the guy's jacket.

Parker trotted forward, the Bobcat in his hand in-side his pocket. The driver, with his Terrazza be-tween him and the action, drew a pistol and yelled at McWhitney, "Hold it! Hold it!" He fired the pistol, not to hit anybody but to attract attention, which he did, from everywhere on the lot.

"Not the model!" yelled the salesman. "Not the model!" Behind him the workman stood, bewildered, the front license plate and a screwdriver in his hands. People everywhere on the lot were craning their necks, trying to see what was going on.

McWhitney was having trouble with the bulky guy. The two of them were struggling over the gun, still half in the guy's jacket pocket.

Parker knew he was too far away with this little gun, but he aimed and fired the Bobcat, then hurried for-ward again. He almost missed completely, but he saw it sting the bulky guy's left ear, making him first lose his concentration on McWhitney and then lose the gun.

It was the same one Parker had taken from him last night, which McWhitney had put in the glove compart-ment of the van. Now McWhitney clubbed the guy with it and, as he fell, stooped and fired one shot through both backseat windows of the Terrazza and into the driver, who dropped backward, his own gun skittering away.

"NOT THE MODEL!"

McWhitney shoved the salesman back into the workman, and both fell down, as he jumped behind the wheel of the Suburban. He had to back around the Terrazza to get away from the building, as Sandra in the Honda stopped beside Parker, who slid aboard. The two men McWhitney had clubbed were both moving; the one he'd shot was not.

With people all around yelling and waving their arms and jumping out of the way, McWhitney slashed through the lot and bumped out to the roadway, forcing a place for himself in among the traffic already there. Demurely, Sandra and the Honda trailed after.

14

Traffic on this commercial road, headed straight south across the Island, was fairly heavy, which meant no one could get much of an edge. Parker could see the black Suburban most of a long block ahead of them, seven or eight cars between, with no way to close the gap. Then the Suburban went through a yellow light, the traffic behind it stopped, and Parker watched the Suburban roll on out of sight.

Was there any pursuit? He twisted around to look out the Honda's rear window just in time to see the Terrazza make the left at the intersection behind them, the lack of glass in its back side window obvious even at this distance. "They're up," he said.

Sandra looked in her mirror, but too late. "Who's up?"

"Somebody in the Buick. One or both of those guys are still in play."

"But they turned off?"

"They know this part of the Island, and they know where McWhitney's headed. They'll get there first."

"And we're too far back to let him know."

"We'll just go to his place and see what happens,"

McW and its entire block were dark, though there were lights on in some of the apartments above the stores. There was no traffic and no pedestrians in this part of Bay Shore at nine o'clock on a Tuesday night. But a black Suburban with a missing front license plate was parked in front of the bar. The white Buick Terrazza was nowhere in sight, but if they'd gotten here before McWhitney they would have tucked it away somewhere.

Parker and Sandra left the Honda and went over to McW. The green shade was pulled down over the glass of the entrance door and the CLOSED sign was in place. Deeper in the bar, the faint nightlights were lit, but that was all.

Parker listened at the door, but heard nothing. They had to be inside there, but somewhere toward the back.

He turned to her. "You got lockpicking tools?"

"It would take a while," Sandra said, looking at the door. "And what if somebody comes along?"

"Not for here, for the back," Parker nodded at

the alley beside the building. "And we'll need a flashlight."

"Can do."

They went back to her car, and from the toolbox next to the accelerator she removed a black felt bag of locksmith's tools, plus a narrow black flashlight.

Parker said, "You know how to use those?"

"I took a course," she said. "It's standard training in my business. Show me the door."

Parker led the way down the alley and around to the back, where the pickup truck could barely be made out in the thick darkness. Faint illumination from the sky merely made masses of lighter or darker black.

"I'll hold the light," he said. "The door's over here."

He held the flashlight with fingers folded over its glass, switched on the light, then separated his fingers just enough to let them see what they needed to see. Sandra went down to one knee and studied the lock, then grunted in satisfaction, and opened the felt bag on the stone at her feet. Then she looked up. "What's the other side of this?"

"His bedroom. They're most likely farther to the front, the living room. More comfortable."

"Not for Nelson," she said, and went to work with the picks from the felt bag.

It took her nearly four minutes, and at one point

she stopped, sat back on her heels, and said, "I am rusty, I must admit. I took that course a while ago."

"Can you get it?"

"Oh, sure. I'm just not as fast as I used to be."

She bent to the lock again, Parker keeping the narrow band of light on her tools, and at last, with a slight click, the door popped a quarter inch toward her. That was the other part of the fire code: exit doors had to open outward.

While she put her tools away, Parker pulled the door a little farther open, pocketed the flashlight, put the Bobcat in his hand, and eased through. Sandra rose, put the felt bag in her pocket, brushed the knees of her slacks, and followed. Now her own pistol was in her hand.

Voices sounded, and then a strained and painful grunt. The bedroom door, opposite them, was partly open, showing one side of the kitchen, the room illuminated only by the lights and clocks on the appliances. The sounds came from beyond that, the living room.

Parker went first, silently crossing the room toward the kitchen doorway. Sandra followed, just behind him and to his right, so that she and her pistol had a clear view in front.

They stepped through into the kitchen. The sounds came from the living room, lit up beyond the next doorway, but only one vacant corner of it visible from here. Parker skirted the table in the middle of the room, and made for that doorway.

"You cocksucker, you make us mad, we *won't* split with you." It was the bulky guy's voice.

"Yeah." A second man, probably the other one in the Buick.

More sounds of beating, and then the bulky guy, exasperated, said, "We're trying to be decent, you son of a bitch. You're *gonna* tell us, and what if we're mad at you then?"

There was no talk for a few seconds, only the other sounds, and then the bulky guy said, "Now what?"

"He passed out."

"Get some water from the kitchen, throw it on him."

Parker gestured for Sandra to stay back, and stood beside the doorway. The Bobcat was too small to hold by the barrel and use the butt as a club, so he simply raised it above his head with the butt extending just a little way below his fingers. When the other one came through the doorway, Parker clubbed straight down at his head, meaning to next step into the doorway and shoot the bulky guy.

But it didn't work. The Bobcat was an inefficient club, and his own fingers cushioned the blow. Instead of dropping down and away, leaving the doorway cleared for Parker, he lurched and fell leftward, toward Parker, who had to push him away with his left hand and club again with his right, this time back-handed, scraping the butt across the bridge of his nose.

The guy crashed to the floor, at last out of the way, but when Parker took a quick look into the living room the moment was gone. McWhitney was slumped in a chair from the kitchen, tied to the chair with what looked like extension cords. The bulky guy was out of sight. Was he in some part of the living room Parker couldn't see, or farther away, in the bar?

The guy on the floor was dazed, but moving. "Mike!" he called. "Mike!"

"Who the hell is it?" The question came from the corner of the living room down to the right of the doorway.

The one on his back on the floor skittered away until his head hit the stove, while he called, "It's the guy killed Oscar!"

"And who else?"

"Some woman."

Parker moved along the kitchen wall toward the spot where Mike would be just on the other side.

"Mike! He's gonna shoot through the wall!"

Parker looked at him. "I don't need you alive," he said.

The guy on the floor lifted his hands, offering a deal. "We can all share," he said. "That's what we were trying to tell your pal there."

Sandra said, "Make him come over here."

Parker nodded. "You heard her."

"No," the guy said.

"You go over there, you live," Parker told him. "You stay where you are, you die."

The guy started to roll over.

"No," Parker said. "You can move on your back. You can get there." Over his shoulder to Sandra, he said, "This is taking too long."

She said, "Don't kill anybody unless you have to."

"I think I have to," Parker said.

"Mike!" cried the guy on the floor. "Mike! What the hell are you doing?"

That was a good question. Parker went to the doorway, flashed a quick look through, then had to duck back again when Mike fired a fast shot at him, very loud in this enclosed space, the bullet smacking into the opposite wall. But in that second what he saw was that Mike had pulled the extension cords off McWhitney, and had the groggy McWhitney sagging on his feet with Mike's left arm around him to hold him as a shield.

Parker looked again and Mike was dragging McWhitney backward toward the door to the bar. He didn't waste a shot in Parker's direction this time, but called, "You come through this door, you're dead," then backed through the doorway, shoved McWhitney onto the floor on this side of it, and slammed the door shut.

Parker turned on the one on the floor. "The money?"

Now that Mike had quit him, the guy was trying to figure out how to change sides, "in the bar," he said. "He carried the boxes in before we jumped him."

Parker turned to Sandra. "You let this thing move," he told her, "I'll kill *you*."

"I'll kneecap him twice," Sandra offered.

But Parker was already on his way, back through the bedroom and out the door to the darkness. He found his way down the alley to the street, turned toward the bar, and its door was propped open, Mike just carrying the first carton of money out, in both arms.

Parker stepped forward and pushed the barrel of the Bobcat into Mike's breadbasket. He fired once, and there was very little noise. "It works," he said, and Mike, eyes and mouth open, darkness closing in, fell down, and back into the bar. Parker kicked his legs out of the way, pulled the liquor carton full of money back inside, and shut and relocked the door.

Going through the bar to the apartment, he stopped in the living room to pick up the extension cords Mike had used to truss McWhitney and brought them to the bedroom, where nothing had changed. Tossing the extension cords onto the floor next to the guy, Parker said to Sandra, "Tie him up. Let's get this over with."

Sandra put her pistol away. "On your stomach. Hands behind your back." As he did so, and she went to one knee beside him, she said to Parker, "What about the other one?"

"He wasn't so lucky."

"Jeeziz," said the guy on the floor.

"Stay lucky," Sandra advised him. When she was satisfied he wasn't going anywhere, she stood and said, "What now?"

"Let's see what Nels looks like."

He didn't look good, but he looked alive, and even groggily awake. The two guys working him over had been eager but not professional, which meant they could bruise him and make him hurt, but couldn't do more permanent damage unless they accidentally killed him. For instance, he still had all his fingernails.

Parker lifted him to his feet, saying, "Can you walk?"

"Uuhh. Where . . ."

With Parker's help, McWhitney walked slowly toward the bedroom, as Parker told him, "One of them's dead in the bar, the other one's alive right there. Tomorrow, you can deal with them both. Right now, you lie down. Sandra and me'll split the money and get out of here."

He helped McWhitney to lie back on the bed, then

said to Sandra, "If we do this right, you can get me to Claire's place by two in the morning."

"What a good person I am," she said.

"If you leave me here," the guy on the floor said, "he'll kill me tomorrow morning."

Parker looked at him. "So you've still got tonight," he said.